Thomas Sherlock

The Life of Charles Stewart Parnell

.

Thomas Sherlock

The Life of Charles Stewart Parnell

ISBN/EAN: 9783337054014

Printed in Europe, USA, Canada, Australia, Japan

Cover: Foto ©Raphael Reischuk / pixelio.de

More available books at **www.hansebooks.com**

THE LIFE

OF

CHARLES STEWART PARNELL,

WITH

AN ACCOUNT OF HIS ANCESTRY.

BY THOMAS SHERLOCK.

WITH

AN APPENDIX,

CONTAINING MOST INTERESTING DETAILS OF C. S. PARNELL'S
EARLY LIFE, AND OF THE PARNELL, STEWART,
AND TUDOR FAMILIES.

BOSTON:
MURPHY & McCARTHY, PUBLISHERS,
33 BROMFIELD STREET.
PROVIDENCE, R.I.: 269 WESTMINSTER ST.
1881.

PRINTED BY DUFFY, CASHMAN & CO.
603 Washington St., Boston.

THE LIFE

OF

CHARLES STEWART PARNELL, M.P.

BEFORE sketching the career of Mr. Parnell from his birth to the present hour, we deem it proper to give some account of the sources whence he sprang. It will be found that on the maternal as well as on the paternal side he had a distinguished ancestry; the former being as noted for honest, hearty hate of English oppression and love of domination as the latter for sincere and practical Irish patriotism.

The story we have to tell must naturally possess a powerful interest for the Irish people; but even if Charles Stewart Parnell were not so endeared to them as he is, the record would have intrinsically a strong attraction for every reader, for it deals with a number of people eminent or illustrious in their day, some of whom played leading parts on the world's great stage, and some, again, about whose lives there is all the brilliancy of romance. In this latter category stands the Irish-American Admiral Stewart, whose daring and successful exploits on the ocean, in especial against the British in the war of 1812, were extraordinary, and whose splendid

career will be traced with considerable fulness of
detail in a subsequent paper. Another of Mr.
Parnell's maternal ancestors, Judge Tudor, took
a stern part against the British in the American
war of independence ; so that we have the interesting fact that the gallant member for Meath has
in his veins the blood of men who fought against
England in the two wars between that country
and the United States. We may add here that
the facts we shall set down will be drawn from
authentic sources, many of which are not generally available.

Beginning with the Parnells, we must say at the
outset that they were originally an English family,
settled for many centuries in the neighborhood
of Congleton in Cheshire. Whatever English
prejudices concerning Ireland they may have had
at first they soon lost ; the English sympathies
they must have brought with them in the beginning grew more and more modified as generation
after generation intermarried in Ireland, until at
length the family obtained renown for its Irish
patriotism.

Strange it is, but true, that many of our most
honored patriots of the past—the men whose
memory the Irish people will ever cherish and
reverence—sprang originally from the alien race.
They saw the great mass of the people ground
into powder, and at the same time cut off from
their natural leaders by the infamous penal laws ;

and with generous hearts aflame with indignation they sprang to the front, and thought, wrote, spoke, fought, and died in the effort to right Ireland's wrongs. So we had Tones and Emmets, Shearoses and Fitzgeralds, leading the people, when O'Briens and MacCarthys, Kavanaghs and O'Neills were hidden away in enforced obscurity. Times have changed since then, and numbers of men of the old race have taken and are taking the part that befits them in the front rank of our political life ; but deep down in Ireland's grateful heart—rooted, fixed, immovable—is the passionate recollection of services rendered and sacrifices made in her cause by so many whose ancestors of a few generations before were as English as the towers of Windsor Castle. Never again will it be possible to create disunion, as in former days, between "the old Irish" and "the new Irish." The unalterable creed of our people is the creed so well preached by Thomas Davis :—

> " Yet start not, Irish-born man —
>   If you're to Ireland true,
>   We heed not blood, nor creed, nor clan—
>   We have no curse for you.

> " And oh! it were a gallant deed
>   To show before mankind
>   How every race and every creed
>   Might be by love combined —
>   Might be combined, yet not forget
>   The fountains whence they rose
>   As filled by many a rivulet
>   ' The stately Shannon flows."

The founder of the Parnell family in Ireland was one Thomas, who came over from Cheshire about the time of the restoration of the Stuart dynasty to the British throne in the person of Charles the Second.

Thomas Parnell bought an estate in the Queen's County, and so came by it in an honester way than three-fourths of the ancestors of the present landed proprietors of Ireland. He throve on this estate; his affairs prospered; and he gave an excellent education to his two sons, John and Thomas, whom he respectively devoted to law and the Church.

John, the younger, who finally came into the family estates, both in Ireland and England, was a man of ability and prominence in his day. He attained a seat in the Court of Queen's Bench, and died, leaving behind him accumulated property.

The parson was also a man of much ability, and enjoyed, not only in his own day, but even up to a generation ago, considerable renown as a poet. He was also a scholar and a wit. He was born in Dublin in 1669, and educated at Trinity College, where he took his degree of M. A. in 1700. Three years afterwards he was ordained; and in 1705 he received the appointment of Archdeacon of Clogher. But his predilections leaned more towards literary work than to ministerial duties, and he preferred to mingle with Swift and Addison, Steele, Congreve, and Pope, in the warm

London coffee-houses, than to mumble through written-out homilies in the cold church of Clogher. Some excuse may be found for him, however; for, although he was probably never reduced to the extremity of his friend Dean Swift at Laracor, when, unable truthfully to begin his sermon with the formal "Dearly beloved brethren," he commenced his address to his sole listener, the parish clerk, with the famous "Dearly beloved Roger," Parson Parnell's congregation must of necessity have been scanty. So in London he spent much of his time, writing poems of a highly moral tendency, as befitted a preacher of the Gospel, occasionally trying his hand at prose, but more often revelling in the enjoyment of the brilliant conversation of the wits with whom he mixed.

His wife, a lady celebrated both for her beauty and her amiability, died after a union with him of but seven years. He never recovered from the blow. Thenceforth, to the end of his own life, he was subject to fits of despondency, and generally shunned the gay society in which formerly he had taken such keen delight. Dean Swift obtained for him the living of Finglas, near Dublin, and so added another to the literary attractions and memories which, through Steele, Addison, Tickell, Sheridan, Delany, and Swift himself, surround the neighborhood of the old hamlet of Glasnevin.

Dr. Thomas Parnell died at a comparatively early age, on his way from London to Ireland, in the ancient city of Chester, in 1717. His remains were interred in one of the churches of the place of his death. He was only in his thirty-eighth year, and had survived his wife but for half a decade. He had issue; but his branch of the Parnell family soon died out. Among his prose works was the "Life of Homer" which was prefixed to the poet Pope's translation of the Iliad. Pope held Parnell in high honor, and after his death edited an edition of his poems. Other poets joined in applauding him. Oliver Goldsmith wrote of him that "his language is the language of life, conveying the warmest thoughts in the simplest expressions." The Scotch poet, Campbell, still more laudatory, says of Parnell's poetry that "its compass is not extensive, but its tone is peculiarly delightful, from the graceful and reserved sensibility that accompanied his polished phraseology." And he adds: "The studied happiness of his diction does not spoil its simplicity. His poetry is like a flower that has been trained and planted by the skill of the gardener, but which preserves, in its cultured state, the natural fragrance of its milder air." Even Dr. Johnson joined in the chorus of praise, saying of Parnell that "he is sprightly without effort, and always delights, though he never ravishes;" and further observes concerning some of his poems: "It is impossible to say whether they are the productions of nature so excellent as not to want the help of art, or of art so refined as to resemble nature." With this brief notice we must be content to part from the one bard of the Parnell family.

John, the judge, was more fortunate with regard to posterity than his brother. He left behind him a son — another John — from whom descended a line of illustrious men. First there was this latter John, who sat in the Irish House of Commons as member for Maryborough for several successive Parliaments. He is described as "a man of great integrity and most amiable character." The "great integrity" was undoubtedly hereditary in the family, as we shall see; the "amiability" has descended too, with this difference — that it is not unvarying or unalterable, but is at times considered very much out of place, more especially in the British House of Commons.

John, the judge, had settled at Rathleague in Queen's County; and, as previously intimated, had left his son a man of good estate. This latter, the member for Maryborough, married in 1744 into a family which, if names are to be relied on, must have been of tolerably pure Gaelic blood. His spouse was Anne Ward, daughter of Michael Ward, of Castle Ward, county Down. Those Wards were by no means ashamed of their Irish name, as is proved by the fact that they bestowed it on their residence. The Wards of Castle Ward were people of consequence in their

day ; a brother of Mrs. Anne Parnell having been
created Lord Bangor.   Her husband, too, — the
" man of great integrity " — must have been a man
of ability also, and have "done the State some
service," for we find that he was created a baronet
in the year 1766, and was thenceforth entitled to
be addressed as " Sir John."

Sir John had a son, also christened John, concerning whom more must be said than of his
father.   While the father sat as member for Maryborough, the son entered the House of Commons
in Collegegreen as member for Bangor.   Both,
in fact, were striving together to serve their
country in a public capacity — and by this time
the Parnells had learned to think no country in
the world as theirs but Ireland.

The son was a remarkable man.   He had a
genuine talent for business ; and as the circumstances of the family forbade its exercise in the
paths of commerce, he gave the full benefit of it
to his land.   In public speaking he never at-
tempted to be rhetorical ; at a time when Irish
Parliamentary orators sought after brilliant periods and pointed epigrams and flashing images,
this John Parnell, of whom we now speak, was
content to say out his thoughts plainly, without
straining after ornament.   Wholly unaffected in
feeling, he was satisfied with " correct language
and a delivery close to his subject ; " and indeed
seems to have concerned himself more with the

matter than the manner of his speeches — to have
been more solicitous to have something weighty
to say than as to the way in which he said it.   He
is described as being a man of "blunt honesty,
a strong discriminating mind, and good talents."

His father — the "man of great integrity" —
died in the year of the declaration of the independence of the Irish Parliament, 1782, and left
him in turn "Sir John."   This second Sir John
was colonel of a regiment of the famous Volunteers of '82, and at a very early stage of the movement for independence both himself and his corps
adopted it zealously and strenuously.   He clung
to it without swerving till his last breath, though
he had the misfortune to live to see the unforgiv-
able crime of the Union accomplished.   After the
death of his father he became member for Queen's
County, for which he was elected again and again
until the extinction of the native Parliament in
which he had labored so long and so honestly.

From an early period of his career he was
selected for the holding of office.   In 1780, while
yet plain John Parnell, he was appointed a com-
missioner of the revenue ; he was made a privy
councillor in 1786 ; and in 1787, when the Right
Honorable John Foster — another firm opponent
of the Union — vacated the post of Chancellor of
the Exchequer to take up that of Speaker of the
Irish House of Commons, Sir John Parnell succeeded him in the Chancellorship.   In this posi-

tion he took an honest, independent part as a
member of the Ministry, and devoted himself with
zeal to the furthering of practical measures to forward the prosperity of his native land.   He
lightened the burden of taxation on the people;
he limited the pension list so that the Government
were hampered in buying disgraceful political service at the expense of the country; he secured a
favorable commercial treaty with France to the
great advantage of Irish trade; and he promoted
the canal system at home for the better develop-
ment of our industrial resources — very creditable
work indeed for the eleven years during which he
held the seals of the Chancellorship.

He seems to have been so immersed in his useful projects as not to have given requisite care to
the consideration of the larger and wider political
principles which were then being enunciated in
Ireland.   Fatal fault!   Reform would have saved
our Parliament, yet Sir John Parnell continued to
hold his position in the Ministry that refused Reform, he dreaming, apparently, that inattention to
the question could never surely pave the way for
the overthrow of the native legislature he so highly prized.   He was destined to a rude awakening.

After the collapse of '98, when the country lay
bleeding, bound, and helpless at the feet of wicked,
rampant, and unscrupulous power, Sir John Parnell was sent for, and the project of the Union
broached to him.   His advice, forsooth, on the

question was first requested. He gave it promptly — gave it firmly — gave it inflexibly. It would
be a ruinous measure for Ireland.

The villain Castlereagh was much concerned at
Sir John's attitude. His personal influence in the
House of Commons was great, on account of his
admitted honesty, judgment, and talents. His
secession from the Ministry would of necessity
weaken it. Besides, he represented at least two
unpurchasable votes; for, having married early
in life a daughter of the Right Hon. Arthur Brooke,
he had now a son, Henry, standing beside him on
the floor of the House as member for Maryborough,·
and possessed of as much integrity and firmness
of purpose as any of his predecessors. Castlereagh was at length reduced to his last shift with
Sir John Parnell, who was left the option of "re-
vising his opinions" with regard to the destruction
of the Irish Parliament, or relinquishing his post
with its honors and emoluments, and the certain
prospect of elevation to the peerage — the post,
too, in which he had already been enabled to do
so much for the good of his fellow-countrymen.

It was not in the nature of Sir John Parnell to
hesitate before such a choice. He honestly believed
a free legislature to be necessary for Ireland's weal,
so he abandoned his office, turned his back on its
advantages, crossed the floor of the House, and
flung himself into the ranks of the patriotic Oppo-

sition, where in the debates on the Union question he did effective service.

Sir John Parnell's constituents of Queen's County presented him with an address approving of his conduct. The address was dated the 18th January, 1799, and was signed on behalf of the electors by the high sheriff of the county. In it they remarked that although he had been a member of the Ministry they had such unbounded confidence in his honor that they did not hesitate to elect him three times in succession, and that now he had proved to them that that confidence was justified. In his reply he promised to continue his opposition to the Union project "as a measure which seems to me more likely to endanger than to give strength to the State" — the State that was in his thoughts being Ireland of course. He declined to allow any weight to the arguments in favor of the Union frequently advanced from the legislative union between Scotland and England. He admitted no analogy between the cases. "Scotland," he said, "in respect to its commerce, was sure of advantages, and did not then risk an extensive trade such as Ireland possesses."

The merchants and traders of Dublin city — most of them Orangemen, be it remembered — were delighted with his spirited behavior; and they too approached him with a highly complimentary address, in which they alluded to his expulsion from the Ministry. In reply to them he said with quiet dignity: "As to my personal situation I acquiesce under it without any adverse feeling. The regards of the most respectable and the most honorable members of the community are a better foundation of honest pride than rank and emolument."

The Maryborough yeomanry, of which he was captain, "added their tribute of respect and congratulation," and presented him with a sword of honor, "as a testimony," they said, "of your dignified and independent principles and conduct." He told them in return that he would be proud to wear that sword in defence of their king, "and of his kingdom of Ireland."

To the last Sir John Parnell and his son Henry actively opposed the Union, both in the House of Commons and elsewhere. Others who began on their side of the question grew weak and accepted bribes, either in place, pension or title, until the farce of carrying the odious measure by a purchased majority was gone through in 1800. But, whoever might waver, the two Parnells would not. They stood firm and unbending to the end, untempted by the golden showers rained from the Treasury, unallured by the coronet that would gladly have been offered as the wages of degradation — indeed as a cheap recompense for their betrayal of their country.

Sir Jonah Barrington contributes the following testimony to Sir John Parnell's character, and it

is all the higher when we remember how at that
period politicians of all shades, both in England
and Ireland, strove to divert as much as possible
of the public revenue into the pockets of themselves or their relations: "Though many years
in possession of high office and extensive patronage, he showed a disinterestedness almost unparalleled; and the name of a relative or a
dependent of his own scarcely in a single instance
increased the place or the pension lists of Ireland."
In Grattan's Life his character is described thus :
"An honest, straightforward, independent man,
possessed of considerable ability and much public
spirit; . . . amiable in private, mild in disposition, but firm in mind and purpose."

After the Union Sir John was sent to the London House of Commons by his old constituency,
the electors of the Queen's County. But he did
not long survive his country's Parliament. Death
seized him, without much warning, on the 5th December, 1801, in London. He was succeeded in
the title and estates by his son, Henry, whose
career was also a very distinguished one, and
highly honoring to himself. He entered the
British Parliament as member for the Queen's
County in 1802, and while there was always the
staunch friend of the oppressed Catholics.

All the members returned to the London Parliament from Ireland—even those who had been
most devoted to their native legislature, and who

had striven hardest against its extinction — accepted in quiet their new position. Grattan himself, though he advised his countrymen to "keep knocking at the Union" in the hope of demolishing it, never dreamt that the place where the hardest knocks of all could be given was in the London Parliament itself. It never occurred to him that by using his great powers towards the hampering of every proceeding of that institution he could offer to the British only a choice between the disintegration of their own legislature, or the restoration of the Irish one. Yet nothing seems more likely than that if the Irish representation as a whole had behaved, from the very beginning in 1801, as a foreign substance introduced into the imperial body, rankling in it more and more as time went on, straitening it in its every action, making it feel sore at every movement, the British would very soon have been heartily sick of the Union, and been glad to submit to the one operation that alone would relieve them from the inflaming foreign substance. Of course, in following this line, the Irish members, to be successful, should have acted with prudence as well as firmness, and, while availing themselves of every Parliamentary privilege, should have been careful to keep well within Parliamentary rules; but want either of tact or of courage was not characteristic of the Irish gentlemen of the beginning of the present century, unless the records of the

2

time misrepresent them much. Indeed, it required no greater degree of those qualities to be
generally antagonistic and troublesome than it did
to face, on numerous special occasions, the angry
demon of English bigotry on the Catholic question ; yet several Irish members did so face it,
and among them one of the foremost was Sir
Henry Parnell.

Sir Henry Parnell's instincts and convictions
were all towards liberal ideas. From a very early
period of his career he espoused the cause of his
downtrodden Catholic countrymen with the ardor
and honesty of his family. His pen as well as
his voice he laboriously exerted in their behalf.
It is hardly possible to exaggerate the beneficial
effect on the cause of Emancipation, produced by
his "History of the Penal Laws" and his "Historical Apology for the Irish Catholics." A Protestant himself, and one whose honor and disinterestedness were beyond question by even the
most malignant bigot, his powerful arrays of facts
supporting his strong arguments must have converted many a sturdy but honest foe into a friend
of the Catholic claims. In the British House of
Commons also, he took every opportunity of
speaking on behalf of his Catholic countrymen's
rights. He was the constant ally of Grattan and
Plunket in the many debates raised from time to
time on the Catholic. question in that House.
Every one knows that it was the mass of the Irish

people under O'Connell, who in the end overthrew the stronghold of British bigotry; yet sight should not be lost of the fact that the three Irish Protestants just named, in conjunction with some others and some liberal-minded English ones, made the first sharp assaults, took the formidable outworks, and undermined the massive walls. Though the details of their efforts be not now generally remembered—though, in fact, there be tens of thousands in Ireland who have never even heard of their endeavors—one remarkable consequence of those and like generous efforts unalterably remains. There is no office of trust or honor in the gift of Irish Catholics to which an Irish Protestant may not aspire, in the full confidence that it will be given to him as freely as if he worshipped in the same temple as they, provided only that he show himself a true Irishman.

One particular hardship pertaining to the lot of Irish Catholics excited Sir Henry Parnell's deepest pity for the victims, and his warmest indignation against the intolerable oppression—the tithe system. Pressed to the very earth by the exactions of his landlord—often reduced, after all his unending toil from year's end to year's end, to subsist on a scanty portion of the humblest fare, to live in a hovel not a whit better than a pigsty, and to clothe himself in a raiment of tatters such as the ragman would not touch with his crook, much less put into his bag—the

peasant had still to support in idleness and lux-
ury the parson whose ministrations he utterly
rejected, and whose teachings he declined without thanks. The parson, on his part, sought his
"tithes" much as a wolf seeks its prey, and commonly seemed to take a fiendish pleasure in adding every circumstance of aggravation to the
collection of the hateful impost. Sir Henry Parnell beheld all this, and his heart was wrung with
compassion, his soul was moved with righteous
wrath. With pains and labor he gathered revolting instances of the shocking oppressiveness of
the tithe exaction, and brought them before the
British House of Commons. He exposed the
rapacity of numerous clergymen of the established Church in regard to tithes; held up to
public execration the diabolical ingenuity which,
by the addition of legal costs, ran up the sum for
which the peasant was liable to five or six times
its original amount; he showed the monstrosity
of having the tithe-claimers themselves the judges
of their own cases against the peasantry in "the
bishop's court;" and denounced the glaring
wickedness of parsons like the one who dis-
trained five sheep from a farmer for a tithe of
five shillings, and bought them in himself afterwards, under the distress, for a shilling apiece.
As with Emancipation, so with tithes—it was
the Irish people themselves who overturned the
abominable system at last; but the task was ren-

dered easier for them by Sir Henry Parnell; his
battering rams had shaken the citadel of iniquity
to its foundations, and but that it was buttressed
by the combined aristocratic and ecclesiastic
power of England it must have fallen before their
shocks.

Both before and after Emancipation Sir Henry
was in general politics what used to be called a
Radical. Taught, probably, by his experience of
the Irish Parliament, he was devoted to reform
of the English one. He lived to become a peer
of Great Britain; but all his life he was heart
and soul a democrat. He was one of the men
who are said to be in advance of their time, but
whose life-labors are nevertheless fruitful for
those who come after them. Among the projects
he advocated in the British House of Commons
were the abolition of all laws restricting either
labor or capital, including the abolition of the
corn laws which made the food of the people
dear; the removal of all unequal taxes, and the
substitution of a property tax; the shortening of
the term for which members of Parliament are
elected, so that constituencies could sooner deal
with those who misrepresent them; an extension
of the franchise; the introduction of the ballot
for the protection of voters from intimidation;
and the abolition of flogging in the army and
navy, and of impressment in the latter. Most of
these projects have since been converted into the

law of the British empire; and so lately as 1879
Mr. C. S. Parnell carried into effect one of the
leading ideas of his far-seeing and reforming relative by virtually "killing the 'cat.'"

The English people, as well as the Irish, have
much for which to thank Mr. C. S. Parnell; and
the case is exactly like with Sir Henry. He it
was who opened for them the way to a reform
of their Parliament. William the Fourth came
to the British throne in the August of 1830.
His Prime Minister was the Duke of Wellington;
his Chancellor of the Exchequer Sir Robert Peel.
On the 12th of November Sir Henry Parnell
moved a resolution—"That a select committee
shall be appointed to take into consideration the
estimates and amounts proposed by command of
his Majesty regarding the Civil List." As a
lively English writer says: "The Civil List is a
list of all the revenues of the Crown—the income
of the king in fact. And here scarcely had his
Majesty got warm in his seat when this audacious
man proposed to overhaul it. His Majesty was
wrathful, and ordered his Ministers to oppose
this daring proposal with all their might. And
this, we may be sure, was done. But, lo! when
the division came off, Sir Henry found that he
had beaten the Government by a majority of
twenty-nine. That was a very great thing to do.
But mark what came of it. The Government
resigned; the reign of Toryism—that 'anarchy

old'—was overthrown at last; and the way was
opened for Earl Grey and Reform. This opened
a new era." It opened a new era for Sir Henry
Parnell himself also; for he was made Secretary
for War in Lord Grey's Government, and Pay-
master-General of the Forces in Lord Mel-
burne's. After thirty-nine years of membership
in the House of Commons he was transferred to
the Lords under the style and title of Baron Congleton. Mental overwork and illness brought on
delirium, in 1842; and on the eighth of June in
that year, at the age of sixty-five, while insanity
obscured his reason, he unfortunately killed himself. He left a son, the second Baron Congleton,
who has at least the merit of voting in favor of
liberal measures.

Sir Henry, like his father, had no pretensions
to oratorical power; but he was admittedly an
excellent debater. He is described towards the
close of his career as "of the middle size, rather
inclining to stoutness; his complexion is fair; his
features are regular, with a mild expression about
them; and his hair is pure white."

Besides Sir Henry, Sir John Parnell left a son,
William, who was content to live the life of a
plain country gentleman, possessed of ample fortune. He had a son, named, after his distinguished
grandfather and uncle, John Henry; and of this
John Henry Parnell Mr. Charles Stewart Parnell, M.P., is the fourth son.

Though this branch of the Parnell family was the younger, it was well endowed with worldly means, and had near aristocratic connections. Neither William nor John Henry was distinguished in the political world; but tradition says that as landlords their relations with their tenantry were of the most satisfactory kind. They would seem, too, to have cherished some pride in connection with the era of Irish independence, to judge from the care with which certain flags of the Volunteers of '82 have been handed down—flags which at present grace C. S. Parnell's mansion of Avondale, near Rathdrum, county Wicklow.

, One of these most interesting relics of a glorious episode in Irish history is a cavalry ensign, of thick silk, richly ornamented on both sides. In shape it is of the kind known as a burgee—that is, an oblong flag with a trangular piece taken from its outer edge. On one side the color of the ensign is red, and on the other yellow. Its dimensions are three feet by two. In a centre-piece on one side appears a dog, with, divided above and below it, the inscription, "Velox et acer—et fidelis amicis," which means, "Swift and sharp—and faithful to friends." Divided above and below the border of the centre-piece is the further inscription, "Independent Wicklow —Fors. Lt. Drags."; which last we take to represent "Foresters' Light Dragoons." On the obverse is an oval centre-piece depicting a harp with

crown surmounting a massive castellated structure ;
and fitted into the corners — a word in each — the
following : "July — Anno — Dom — 1779," showing the date at which the Independent Wicklow
Foresters' Light Dragoons were embodied.   A
similar device to this obverse one is painted on,
not worked into, the other flag, which is a large
infantry ensign of thin silk, now unfortunately
giving way before the ravages of time.

John Henry Parnell, when a young man, went
about seeing the world with his cousin Lord
Powerscourt; and while travelling in America he
met, at Washington, the daughter of Admiral
Stewart, of the American navy.   He made her
acquaintance; they became intimate; an attachment sprang up between them; and after a while
the aristocratically connected young Irishman
took to wife the daughter of the old republican
sea-warrior.   The marriage was solemnized in
New York.   By this step John Henry Parnell
brought into the family the blood of two men who
had dared death in mortal combat with the British
forces, and who, we may be sure, had trans-
mitted to their offspring little love of the power
whom they had considered it a duty and an honor
to oppose even to the shedding of blood.   A man's
marriage is often the most momentous action of
his own life.   In the case of John Henry Parnell
it was large in its consequences to Great Britain
as well as to Ireland; for the issue of his marriage

was five sons and six daughters ; among those sons
was the present virtual leader of the Irish people,
and if the land question of Ireland bids fair to get
a satisfactory settlement largely through his guidance, the Parliament of Great Britain has received
at his hands a shock to its traditions from which
it can but slowly recover, if indeed it ever do recover at all.

At this stage of our record we shall leave the
Parnells for a while, and turn to Charles Stewart
Parnell's maternal ancestry. We shall find in
their history many facts of deep interest.

More than a century ago, a Mr. Stewart, of
Belfast, who was married to a lady whose maiden
name was Sarah Ford, left Ireland in deep disgust
with the state of affairs there, and determined to
settle in what were then called the British colonies
in North America, but which are now infinitely
better known to all the world as the United States.
The Fords, we need hardly observe, were originally a Connaught clan, and of as pure Milesian
blood as any in Ireland. A great number of
Northern Irishmen emigrated to America like Mr.
Stewart about that period, and one and all, as
even Mr. Froude admits, bore with them a burning hate of English misgovernment.

After the Irish fashion, the Stewarts had a large
family. On the 28th of July, 1778, the youngest
of eight children, a son, was born to them in
Philadelphia, but a few weeks over two years sub-

sequent to the famous "Declaration of Independence." This son of Irish parents, overflowing with the vitality of the eternal Celtic race from which he drew his origin, lived to become one of the great naval heroes of history, had a career which cannot be described as anything less than romantic; and died after bearing for seven years the title of "admiral" — he being the very first on whom that title was conferred in the navy of the United States.   Previous to 1862 the designation of the highest rank in that navy was "commodore;" and Admiral Stewart had been so dubbed formally for a great many years.   He was the maternal grandfather of Charles Stewart Parnell. We mean to record his career with some detail; but for the sake of clearness in the general narrative we shall leave him for a little while, and turn for a moment to another branch of C. S. Parnell's maternal ancestry.

At the beginning of the American war of independence there was settled in Boston a young lawyer whose name was Tudor.   A very English name, every reader will exclaim who remembers that it was the family name of the infamous monarch, Henry the Eighth of England.   A very English name it was, in truth.   But Englishmen had been driven from their own land by governmental persecution just as Irishmen had been; all who entertained ideas of liberty, whether in the civil or religious domain, were obnoxious to the powers that were. So it came to pass that hosts of English colonists brought with them from their own to American shores an abiding sense of wrong, and a firm determination to resist any encroachments of the home government on their new-found liberties. Therefore, when this English-descended lawyer found the colonists ready to take up arms for freedom's sake, he was, like the Irish-descended lawyer, John Sullivan, one of the first to declare for it. He joined the army of the immortal Washington, and went through all the perils of the revolutionary war.

In doing so, besides risking life and limb, Tudor sacrificed his tenderest feelings for what he was convinced was his duty. He was ardently attached to a young lady whose people were devoted adherents of the British cause. They were engaged to be married when the civil commotion arose. It opposed a barrier to their union, which would not be allowed because forsooth he was a "rebel" to the British Government. He went on fighting against that Government as if he were wholly indifferent on the subject of the marriage; but after five years, when success was smiling on the cause of the insurgents, it was conveyed to him that all objections would be withdrawn. There are many men who, under like circumstances, would have exhibited the obstinacy of wounded vanity; but Mr. Tudor loved his sweetheart for her gracious self, not for her political notions—whether they happened to be what he thought right or wrong—so he gladly espoused her after their long separation.

The spirit of Judge Tudor was communicated to his offspring; and when, after a generation, the rebellious stream of the Tudor blood was mingled with the fiery, indignant stream of the Stewarts', the mixture was not of a kind very susceptible to impressions favoring the notion that the inhabitants of England are a heaven-ordained governing race.

Admiral Stewart's father had been the master of an American merchant vessel. In less than two years after the birth of his youngest child, Charles, he died. The revolutionary war was still being actively waged, with the natural result of damaging almost every commercial interest in the country. Mrs. Stewart's resources were crippled like those of the mass of her fellow-citizens; and in these circumstances it was no easy matter for the widow to rear and educate eight children. But this daughter of the Fords, who is said to have been a woman of talent and great energy, accomplished her task single-handed for several years. Eventually she gave her children a step-father in the person of Captain Britton, who was a member of Congress, an intimate friend of Washington, and the commander of the body-guard of that most illustrious because most unselfish of successful soldiers. Captain

Britton was fond of young Charles Stewart, took him about with him, and on one occasion, in the presence of both Houses of Congress, introduced the boy, when he was about the age of twelve, to Washington himself. The incident made a deep impression on the youngster's mind. Even in his old age he was fond of recalling it, and used to speak with glee of the effect it had on his Philadelphian playfellows. "Not one of them," he would say, "dared knock a chip off my shoulder after that."

Charley was a wild, courageous boy, and cherished from an early age a positive passion for the sea. It would appear as though his naval aspirations were discouraged in the home circle; for about the age of thirteen he gave his friends the slip, ran away from school, and began his career on the ocean — a career destined to be so glorious — in the very humble capacity of cabin boy on board a merchant vessel. Just two years afterwards he was near losing his life at the hands of a leader of the negro insurgents of Hayti — namely, Christophe, who afterwards became king of the Island. Christophe had been a slave and a tavern-cook; but when the insurrection broke out against the French in San Domingo he joined the insurgents, and partly on account of his enormous stature and great strength, partly by reason of his reckless daring and abundant energy, soon rose to a position of high command. We append a description of the incident above referred to, taken from an old Life of Stewart:—

"The Loraine, owned by Britton and Massey, of Philadelphia, and commanded by Captain Church, came to anchor at St. Domingo, in 1793, just at the time of the insurrection. Charles Stewart was on board, still at the lowest round of the sailor's ladder, for he was only fifteen years old and had been but two years at sea. One day, Christophe, a leader of the insurrectionists, came alongside in a row-boat, with several of his sable followers. The 'citizen-general' was attired in the elegant uniform of a French officer, which illy accorded with his ungainly carriage and bare black feet. Two of the, teeth of his lower jaw protruded like the tusks of an animal, and added to the incongruous and grotesque effect. The awkward rowing of the natives, together with the comical appearance of the magnate, were too much for Charley. When Christophe asked him to throw him something by which to ascend the side of the ship, a spirit of deviltry seized the lad, and instead of tossing the rope to the visitor, he shook it in his face, and burst into a laugh.

"In an instant Charley realized the extent of his offence, and, fearing vengeance, ran towards the cabin for protection. The commodore always said, in telling this story, that while on his way to the cabin 'something told him' that if he went there it would cost him his life. He at once changed his course, hurried to the place where the cook kept his wood, opened the trap-door, and jumping into the hole, replaced the cover and shoved a stick through the ring, so that the door could not be opened from above. He had not been there many minutes when he heard Christophe and his men searching for him overhead.

"It seems that the blacks finally succeeded in getting on board, the leader blind with rage. He demanded that that 'white-headed boy' should be given up to him immediately, and swore that he would have the fellow's life. Captain Church was not sufficiently provided with arms to prevent violence, and pretended to aid him in his quest, after having failed to convince him that the lad had jumped overboard and swam to a French vessel which was lying not far off. Every portion of the Loraine was searched, and the sailors were even compelled to shift a part of the cargo in the hold.

"At last Christophe caught sight of the trap-door, beneath which the boy was lying in a state of fearful suspense. The moment the sailors found that this had been fastened from beneath, they knew that Charley must have made here his hiding-place, and they swore still more stoutly that he had swam to the French vessel. They exerted themselves, however, in fruitless mock efforts to lift the door; but Christophe, not satisfied, thrust his sword down on every side, the blade just escaping young Stewart, who cuddled himself up into small space in the centre.

"At last the search was given up, and the captain, in order to appease Christophe, made him the magnificent present of a pair of stockings. These pleased the savage so that he fairly danced with delight; his good humor was still further augmented by the gift of a pair of shoes. The fellow finally got drunk on their liquors, supplied without stint, and in this condition they succeeded in getting rid of a most unwelcome guest.

" A week or two after this adventure — the ship still remaining at St. Domingo, as it was found difficult to dispose of the cargo in consequence of the disturbed state of affairs — young Stewart resolved to venture ashore. The captain gave him permission, at the same time warning him of his danger. But Stewart thought that, as Christophe had only seen his white head, he could easily disguise himself so that he would not recognize him. Accordingly he put on a different rig, and pulled his hat over his eyes so as to hide his silver-colored hair.

" The very first man he met, in sauntering up the street, was Christophe — French uniform, sword, pistols, musket, tusks, and all. We may be sure that the little fellow's heart sank within him, and that his first impulse was to take to his heels. But the boy's characteristic presence of mind and coolness in the face of danger saved his life. Carelessly whistling a tune, he kept on steadily, and in passing Christophe his clothes actually brushed against him. He felt that the savage had his eye fixed upon him suspiciously; and after passing him heard with affright the click caused by the cocking of a musket. The boy still moved on slowly, and apparently with the utmost unconsciousness; but turning the first corner, he scampered down a side street as fast as his legs could carry him. The rest of the day he lay hidden in the mountains, returning after dark to shore, and finding means to make his way back to the ship."

But if Charley Stewart at the age of fifteen was still only at the foot of the seaman's ladder, he did not long remain so. Before he was yet twenty he had risen, step by step, through every grade of the merchant service, to the command of an India-man — a position almost unparalleled at so early an age. Still Charles Stewart was not content. He wished to devote himself to his country's service ; for the French had made certain demands regarding rights of search and of capture of American vessels which the Government could not but withstand, and the two republics were on the verge of war. Therefore, Charles Stewart sought and found admission to his country's armed navy, and on the 9th of March, 1798, he was duly commissioned a lieutenant of the frigate *United States* commanded by the gallant Wexford man, Commodore John Barry, whose business it was to put an end to the depredations of French privateers on American commerce in the neighborhood of the West Indies.

In little more than two years — to wit, on the 16th of July, 1800 — the young lieutenant received an independent command in the schooner *Experiment*, fourteen guns. His cruising ground was still in the neighborhood of the West Indies. He had now the opportunity of distinguishing himself, and he hastened to avail himself of it.

From a sketch of his life we copy the following summary of his brilliant exploits in the *Experiment:* —

"On the night of the first of September he fell in with, and, after an action of ten minutes, captured the

French schooner, *Deux Amis*, of eight guns, which he
sent home for condemnation. While watering in Prince
Rupert's Bay, in the island of Dominica, two British
sloops of twenty guns each arrived, one having an
American named Amos Seeley impressed among its
crew. Seeley wrote to Stewart imploring his help.
He at once opened a characteristic correspondence with
the British captain, demanding the release of the
American, and in a personal interview with the officer
used such logic as to induce him, although with reluc-
tance, to comply. While cruising at daylight, on the
13th of September, two sails were discovered, bearing
down on the *Experiment*, with the English colors flying.
The *Experiment* was laying to with the British signal
of the day flying. As they refused to answer his signal,
and proved to be a brig of eight guns and a schooner
of fourteen, Stewart determined to try the sailing
qualities of the vessels. Discovering the *Experiment*
could outsail them, they abandoned the chase, running
up the French flag, and firing a gun of defiance to windward. Stewart immediately tacked ship and worked to
windward, and gaining the gauge on them in turn became the pursuer. About three o'clock in the evening
she ranged up on the larboard quarter of the sternmost one and poured a broadside into her. In a few
minutes the schooner struck and surrendered to the
Experiment. She proved to be the French schooner
Diana, on board of which were a lieutenant and a de-
tachment of thirty invalid soldiers, a crew of sixty-
five men, and General Rigaud on his way to France.
Stewart immediately started after the brig, but she had
got safe beyond his reach. After disposing of his
prisoners at St. Christopher, Lieutenant Stewart did

valuable service in protecting American commerce in those seas.

"On the 16th of November, at midnight, he fell in with an armed vessel, which refused to answer his hail. After repeated efforts to learn the character of the stranger, he sent a shot into her, which was answered by a broadside. A running fight of forty minutes ensued, when the unknown struck. She proved to be a privateer of Bermuda, carrying eight guns. She was much cut up in her rigging, and had two shots through her bottom. Stewart lay by all next day assisting in the repair of her damages.

"The *Experiment* being ordered home, Lieutenant Stewart on the voyage rescued sixty-seven persons from a reef off Saona Island, and carried them to their homes in St. Domingo, the Government of which island wrote a warm letter of thanks to President Jefferson."

A reduction of the navy was carried out by the Government in 1801, when only thirty-six out of the whole body of lieutenants were retained in the service. Of these thirty-six Charles Stewart was one. He lost his independent command, however, being appointed first officer in the frigate *Constellation* in 1802. When the vessel returned from her cruise, the war with Tripoli was afoot. In times of strife men like Stewart are properly valued in every navy. This was especially the case in the infant one of the United States. Stewart was at once appointed to the command of a new war-brig, the *Siren*, carrying sixteen guns, and ordered forthwith to join the squadron off the coast of Barbary. Here he was employed blockading Tripoli and the harbors adjacent; in which service he succeeded in capturing a British brig and a Greek vessel. We read, that "on the 3d of August, 1804, the *Siren* led the attack on the town, flotilla, and batteries of Tripoli. For the gallant manner in which Stewart brought his vessel into action and prompt obedience to signals, the commodore the next day in general orders thanked him. For the whole of August and part of September the squadron vigorously bombarded the city and batteries of Tripoli whenever the wind would permit their approach and withdrawal. Upon all such occasions, night or day, they sent their flaming shells or crushing round shots at the foe, sinking several of their flotilla and damaging the batteries and houses." The conclusion of a treaty of peace put an end for the time to Stewart's chances of distinguishing himself further.

So far the incidents of Charles Stewart's naval career were evidences of his gallantry and skill. His next service was one which exhibited in him clear-sightedness, good sense, and highly honorable feeling. He had been promoted to the rank of Master Commandant, put in charge of a thirty-two gun-ship, the *Essex*, and despatched with a squadron to Tunis, between which State and the Union there was trouble brewing. The American consul sought refuge on board the fleet, so hos-

tile was popular feeling among the Tunisians.
The posture of affairs was so serious, we read,
that "a council was convened on board the flag-
ship, the situation was explained, and the opinion
of the officers demanded whether hostilities ought
not to be immediately commenced. Captain
Stewart gave it as his opinion that there was no
power under the constitution which authorized
hostilities and war on others, but that which was
lodged exclusively with Congress; that the President could not exercise this power without the
action and authority of Congress, much less the
commander of an American squadron; that due
respect for the laws of nations forbade aggres-
sion, and only justified self-defence by vigilance
and convoy for the protection of citizens, their
property and commerce; but where hostile at-
tempts were made on either, he would be justified in seizing all persons engaged in them, but
no farther would his country sanction his acts."
His sound reasoning and discretion prevailed,
and amicable relations were soon restored; the
consul returning to his post, and the Bey of
Tunis sending a special Minister to the United
States. When President Jefferson received from
the consul-general a copy of that opinion as delivered to the council, he expressed to his Cabinet
"the high satisfaction he felt at having an officer
in the squadron who comprehended the interna-

tional law, the constitution of his country, and the policy of his Government."

Naturally promotion followed a man who could not only fight and handle a ship, but could think clearly and judiciously for his country's interests and good name as well. A post-captaincy — then the highest rank in the United States navy — was bestowed on him the 22d of April, 1806; and as there was no need to employ him on active service, his versatile talents were turned to account in another way — namely, in superintending, at New York, for a couple of years, the construction of a flotilla of gun-boats.

Several years of peace followed, which Post-Captain Stewart, with the sanction of the authorities, utilized for his own profit in commercial enterprises which added considerably to his means. However, on the breaking out of the war with England in 1812, the first thought of the hero was not for himself or his interests but for his country's. He hastened to Washington to offer his services; but was stunned by receiving, at the navy department, the dismaying intelligence that President Madison's Cabinet, in view of the overwhelming superiority of the British navy, had decided to collect all the Union ships of war in New York harbor, partly to defend the place and partly to save the infant navy from annihilation. Stewart and Captain Brainbridge joined in an effort to convert the Secretary

of the Navy from the holding of a tenet so humil-
iating to the country ; and that same evening they
addressed a joint letter to President Madison, so
spirited, powerful, and convincing "as to cause
him to immediately direct the Secretary of the
Navy to send the vessels of war to sea to seek
their enemy, and he would take the responsibility
on himself." So that, before a shot was fired,
Stewart had already covered himself with glory
by being so deeply instrumental in taking his
country out of a position of disgraceful timidity
and national humiliation. The result fully proved
the wisdom as well as the courage of both Brainbridge and Stewart; for the naval annals of this
war of 1812 are among the brightest records of
heroic feats of arms and marvellous successes of
which Americans can legitimately boast.

The day after the writing of the timely and influential letter just referred to, Stewart received
instructions from the Secretary of the Navy to
proceed immediately to New York to take command of the *Argus*, with which he was to scour
the West Indies and the Gulf Stream, and to
attack and capture every British ship he could,
whether of war or merchandise. In the Secretary's communication occurs the following sentence, so highly flattering to Stewart: "To your
judgment, your valor, and your patriotism is
committed the best course to be pursued to ac-
complish the object of these instructions."

Nevertheless Stewart did not assume command of the *Argus*. A better vessel was put at his disposal. We read : "At a ball given to Captain Stewart and his officers before they proceeded to sea in the *Constellation*, by the citizens of Washington, in December, 1812, about ten o'clock at night, midshipman Hamilton, the son of the Secretary of the Navy, arrived with the flag of the *Macedonian* (British) frigate, and despatches from Captain Decatur, announcing his having captured her with the frigate *United States*. The dancing ceased, the flag was unrolled, and the despatch read to the President and the assembled ladies and gentlemen. The wildest scene of glorious confusion followed. A venerable Senator of the United States embraced the President ; and the Secretary of the Navy, in a spirit of frankness beyond praise, announced to those assembled : 'It is to Captains Brainbridge and Stewart you owe your naval victories.' "

The *Constellation* was the vessel in which Charles Stewart set forth against the British ; but, notwithstanding her starry appellation, her performances were not brilliant on that cruise. It was her gallant commander's ill fortune to be blockaded in the harbor of Norfolk, Virginia, by a fleet of heavy ships belonging to the enemy, against which it would have been sheer madness to dream of contending. But to be inactive at such a crisis in the fortunes of his land was the

idea which of all others he could least entertain.
He accordingly got himself transferred to the
frigate *Constitution*, in which he set sail from Boston in December, 1813, for the West Indies.   In a
short time he had met and destroyed several British ships, including the *Picton*, of sixteen guns, a
privateer of ten guns, a schooner, and a brig.
The *Constitution* had put so hurriedly to sea that
after a few months she had to return to get new
sails, instead of the worn-out ones she carried.
On her way she was chased by two of the enemy's
frigates, and Captain Stewart, not satisfied that
his craft was just then in proper fighting trim,
skilfully gave them the slip, and ran her almost
under the guns of the fort of Marblehead, about
sixteen miles north-east of Boston, where she was
in safety.   In a few days she was able to make
Boston to refit.

It had happened many years previously that in
an idle moment Charles Stewart had submitted to
the imposition of one of that class of frauds
known as "fortune-tellers," by whom he had been
informed that it was his fate to marry "the belle
of Boston."   By one of those singular coincidences which sometimes happen, the prediction
was literally verified.   While waiting for his ship
to be got ready he fell in love with and espoused
Miss Delia Tudor, daughter of the Judge Tudor
before mentioned, and who was pre-eminently
"the belle" of the city.   Short time was allowed

afterwards for nuptial bliss. The *Constitution* was ready for another cruise, and the bridegroom could no longer tarry with his bride. As he parted from her he asked her what present she would like him to bring for her on his return. "Bring me a British frigate," was her patriotic answer. "You shall have two," he replied, his eyes kindling with love and pride; "and I shall wear my wedding uniform in battle."

It was in the December of 1814 that he again put to sea, as little regardful of the Winter's wild storms as of the enemy's countless ships. Two of the latter were soon in his hands. One he destroyed; the other, which had on board a valuable cargo, he sent to New York.

By February, 1815, he was off the coast of Spain. There was some repining among the subordinate officers of the *Constitution* at the ill luck of the vessel in not having had a brush with the enemy off the European coast. Charles Stewart overheard them grumble. Perhaps he had a presentiment of what was about to come; perhaps — and this is more likely — he was actually in search, from information he had picked up, of certain British war-ships in his neighborhood. Whatever his inspiration, it is certain that he bade the officers to keep up their spirits, for the chance of distinguishing themselves for which they sighed was close at hand. "I assure you, gentlemen," he concluded, "that before another sun sets you will be engaged in battle with the enemy, and it will not be with a single ship." This was said on the morning of the 19th of February.

About half-past one o'clock on the same day a sail some twelve miles away was descried by the look-out on the masthead of the *Constitution*. Chase was given until four o'clock, by which time the distance between the vessels was lessened by one-half, when unfortunately, under the power of a freshening breeze, the main-royal mast of the *Constitution* was carried away. Nothing could well be more vexatious to men "spoiling for a fight" as were those on board, since the accident in the short February evening gave the chase an excellent chance of slipping away. However, the gallant captain wasted no time in fretting over the mishap; but got to work at once in repairing the damage, and with such celerity that in half an hour a new spar had been put up, the royal sail again set, and the *Constitution* was forging ahead at her utmost speed. Just at this time another ship of war was reported by the look-out, and evidently exchanging signals with the chase. Captain Stewart understood the signals, and from them divined that the vessels were British men-of-war and consorts. What followed is so well described in the Life of Stewart, from which we have before quoted, that we shall make use of the description here : —

" One of the vessels being painted with double yellow streaks and false ports in the waist, had at a distance the appearance of a double-decked ship, and Lieutenant Ballard told Captain Stewart that she must be at least a fifty-gun ship. He replied that she looked too small to be a ship of that class, but might be an old forty-four on two decks. ' However,' he added, ' be this as it may, you know I promised you a fight before the setting of to-morrow's sun, and if we do not take it now that it is offered, we can scarcely have another chance. We must flog them when we catch them, whether she has one gun-deck or two ! '

" At five o'clock the leeward ship bore up before the wind, under easy sail, to enable the chased ship to join her. The *Constitution* having gained considerably on the chase, with a hope of crippling her, or bringing her to action before she could join her consort, fired a shot at her which fell short. The chase continued until the two ships joined, and a little before seven o'clock, the moon shining brightly, the British ships hauled to the wind in a line ahead of each other, about two hundred yards apart. Reducing to fighting sail, and heaving to with the main-top sails to the masts, they awaited the American's coming up. The *Constitution* was on the starboard quarter of the sternmost vessel, about one mile distant. Furling in all except the topsails, jib, and topgallant sails, reduced to fighting trim, she gradually luffed to starboard, and ranged along the windward side of the sternmost ship until she reached the desired position, which was at the apex of the equilateral triangle, the British ships forming the base line. Stewart heaving the *Constitution* to, with the mainsails to the mast and the jib in brails, he fired a shot, not at either, but between both, with a view to invite the ac-

tion and draw their fire. His motive for this was to
make the British commit the first act of hostility, he
having boarded a Russian ship three days before, direct
from London, and received from her captain a copy of
the London *Times*, containing the heads of the treaty
of Ghent, as signed by the Ministers of the United
States and Great Britain, and said to have been ratified
by the Prince Regent. Supposing the British ships
might have later information than himself, he wished
to give them a chance to decline battle if peace had
been made between the two countries."

Here we may interrupt the narrative for a moment to note how scrupulously Captain Stewart
respected the rules and regulations of naval warfare, or, as it would be phrased in the London
Parliament kept himself "in order." But to continue : —

"The *Cyane* (Captain Gordon Falcon) and the
Levant (Captain Hon. George Douglas) answered
with broadsides and musketry, and the *Constitution*
opened with a division on the gun deck and another on
the forecastle on the *Levant*, and two divisions on the
gun deck and another on the quarter deck on the
Cyane. The *Constitution* maintained the same position
throughout the fight, as a nearer approach would have
thrown one of the ships out of the line of her fire, and
exposed her to being raked. Thus the battle was continued for about forty minutes, when the *Levant* wore
off before the wind and retired from the fight. Her
consort the *Cyane*, immediately after wore short
round, and hauling close to the wind, poured in her

broadside with her colors struck and hanging over the taffrail, as the *Constitution* was in the act of wearing around after her. Not the slightest injury was done by this fire. Stewart, though feeling incensed, did not return it, determined to hold the officer in command responsible. The matter was afterwards explained as occurring in mistake. The *Cyane* was immediately taken possession of, and her officers sent on board the *Constitution*, which filled away to leeward after the *Levant*, followed by the prize, with the American ensign flying. The *Levant*, finding it impossible to escape, wore ship, and ranged under larboard tack along the starboard battery of the *Constitution* in close and gallant style, and delivered her fire. The *Constitution* poured into her a broadside, and wearing short around, plunged into her stern three chase shots, which arrested her escape and brought down her colors. She was immediately boarded and her officers sent to Stewart's ship.

"The principal injury received by the *Constitution* was in her rigging; that of the enemy's ships in their hulls. The Americans had three killed and twelve wounded, three of the latter mortally. The *Cyane* lost twelve killed and twenty-six wounded; the *Levant* twenty-three killed and sixteen wounded — total British casualties, seventy-seven. The *Constitution* mounted fifty-one guns, twenty-four of which were thirty-two pounders; the *Cyane* thirty-two guns, of which twenty-two were thirty-two pounders; and the *Levant* twenty-one guns, eighteen of which were thirty-two pounders. The odds against the *Constitution* is most clearly shown in the calibre of the guns, the British carrying sixteen more thirty-two pounders."

In his History of the American Navy, J. Fen-
nimore Cooper, commenting on this splendid
naval victory, says : —

"The manner in which Captain Stewart handled his
ship on this occasion excited much admiration among
nautical men ; it being unusual for a single vessel to
engage two enemies and escape being raked. So far
from this occurring to the *Constitution*, however, she
actually raked both her opponents ; and the manner
in which she backed and filled in the smoke, forcing
her two antagonists down to leeward when they were
endeavoring to cross her stern or forefoot, is surely
the most brilliant manœuvring in naval annals."

A couple of anecdotes relating to this sea-fight
can hardly fail to be interesting here.

While the victor was sitting in his cabin, talk-
ing with one of his prisoners, a British captain,
there entered a midshipman of the *Contitution*, to
inquire if the crew might have their usual allowance of grog. Now the ordinary time of serving
out grog had passed before the action began ; so
Captain Stewart, in surprise, asked if the men had
not been supplied already. "No, sir," replied
the midshipman ; "it was mixed ready for serving
just before the battle began, but the forecastle
men and other old sailors of the crew said they
didn't want any Dutch courage on board, and capsized the grog-tub in the lee-scuppers." That is
precisely the sort of spirit which at least deserves

success, and which generally succceds in attaining it.

The two British captains were foolish enough to dispute in Stewart's presence concerning the conduct of the battle, and to blame each other for not having done this, that, or the other which must infallibly have brought about a different result to the action. Such paltry endeavors to shift blame from each to the other were eminently distasteful to a truly brave man, as Stewart was; and at length he felt bound to interfere. "Gentlemen," said he, "there is no use in getting warm about it; it would have been all the same whatever you might have done. If you doubt that, I will put you all on board again, and you can try it over." Englishmen would say that the remark was only a specimen of " Yankee bumptiousness ; " impartial critics may see in it merely the confidence of a man who knew why and how he had won, and who felt himself able to do again what he had already done. At all events the British captains did not jump at his offer, but preferred to remain snug and safe as prisoners of war on board the *Constitution.*

On the 10th of March the *Constitution* and her two splendid prizes arrived at Port Praya in the island of Santiago, the largest of the Cape de Verde group. Next day the British captains were allowed on shore, on parole, to make arrangements for the transport of their crews to

Barbadoes. They secured two brigs in the harbor. While the *Constitution's* boats were carrying provisions, etc., to the brigs, a heavy British squadron, under Sir George Collier was discovered approaching in the thick fog, within three miles of the position of Stewart's ship and her prizes. It was the well known policy of the British ships of war to attack their enemy's cruisers in neutral waters if it could be done without danger. They preferred reimbursing any claims made upon such neutral by an enemy than to allow that enemy's vessel to escape and commit depredations upon their commercial marine. Stewart was well aware of this; he appreciated accurately the utterly unscrupulous character of the British; and he instantly recognized the danger of his position. Beating to quarters, making all sail, and cutting cable, he got under way, and stretched out of the harbor, followed by the two prizes. The British fleet hurried immediately in pursuit, the *Acasta*, of fifty guns, gradually crawling up to the prize *Cyane*. Stewart signalled the latter to tack and separate from him, which she did, and doubled their rear, and arrived safe in New York. The fleet held steadily in pursuit of the *Constitution;* the *Newcastle*, sixty-four guns (Captain Lord George Stewart), coming well up. Fortunately, however, she opened fire by divisions, which had the effect of retarding her sailing much. Stewart apprehended most from the posi-

tion and weatherly qualities of the *Acasta*, which
he saw would soon obtain a position to hold the
Constitution in check until her more powerful consort could come up. Fighting was out of the
question, as his crew was short by reason of having to subtract from it the crews which took possession of the prizes; while the crews of the
prizes themselves were of necessity much too weak
to handle those vessels in an encounter with a
powerful squadron. Nothing was left to Commander Stewart, therefore, than to trust to his
skill in manœuvring to get away unscathed. He
consequently signalled the *Levant* to tack, and
lighted his shot-furnace, in the hope of putting a
few red-hot balls into the enemy's hull and setting
her on fire, so forcing her consorts to go to her
relief.

Immediately after the *Levant* tacked, a signal
was thrown out from the *Leander*, the sixty-four
gun ship of Sir George Collier, who commanded
the squadron, for the *Acasta* to tack after the
Levant, and the *Leander* and the *Newcastle* tack-
ing at the same time to cut off her retreat by their
rear, thus compelled the *Levant* to return to Port
Praya, where she anchored under the guns of the
forts, in neutral waters, in which, according to in-
ternational law, she should have been perfectly
safe from attack. The British fleet, however, followed her and entered the harbor, taking her
thence by force with them to the West Indies,

together with the boats of the *Constitution* and
her anchors, and those of the *Cyane* and *Levant*,
left in the neutral waters of the harbor. Not the
slightest attempt was made by the forts to preserve the neutrality of the waters inviolate. The
Portuguese, being weak, were afraid to stand up
for their rights; and the British, who have a
great respect for the strong, and none whatever
for the weak, trampled without scruple, after their
wont, on the undoubted rights of the Portuguese,
simply because they were weak.

Stewart, however, contrived to elude them, and
in the *Constitution* proceeded to Brazil, landed his
prisoners, and returned to Boston. The news of
his remarkable victory was received with enthusiasm throughout the country. In Boston he and
his officers were honored with a triumphal pro-
cession. In New York the council voted him the
freedom of the city, gave him a gold snuff-box,
and him and his officers a public dinner. Penn-
sylvania voted him the thanks of the common-
wealth and a gold-hilted sword. Congress passed
a vote of thanks to him and his brave officers,
caused a gold medal to be struck in his honor,
and presented it to him in commemoration of
the event.

The remainder of Admiral Stewart's career we
condense from an excellent sketch of his life which
appeared in the *Bordentown Register*, and to
which we have been already indebted.

The war having terminated with Great Britain,
Captain Stewart never again met the enemy in
battle. Yet his active career of usefulness in the
service of his country was not ended. In the
Mediterranean squadron, commanded by Commodore Chauncey, a widespread spirit of mutiny had
manifested itself. So far had it gone that the
malcontent officers had actually " threatened to
draw their swords on their commanders." Commodore Stewart was in 1817 sent in ship-of-the-
line *Franklin* to supersede Chauncey and restore
the proper discipline. In 1819 he ordered a
court-martial to meet on board the *Guerriere*, to
try a marine for an alleged offence. The officers,
however, preferred to sit at a hotel in Naples,
where the man was tried and convicted. The
commodore, knowing that the session of the court
at any place than that directed by orders was
illegal, disapproved the proceedings, released the
prisoner, and informed the court of his action.
The court passed a series of resolutions, which act
was instantly followed by the arrest of every commanding officer of the vessels of the squadron.
This summary proceeding at once restored a
healthy state of feeling throughout the squadron.
The President and Cabinet approved of Stewart's
proceeding, but as the officers expressed regret at
their conduct, the matter was dropped.

While the squadron lay at Naples the Emperor
of Austria and suite visited the *Franklin*. The

grand master of the Empress, arrayed in a mag-
nificently brilliant uniform, being somewhat near-
sighted, mistook a wind sail for a mast, and fell
from the deck to the cock-pit, breaking his ankle.
The commodore, who was engaged in conversation
at the time, not seeing what had happened, asked
what the matter was. The old quartermaster of
the watch, whose duty it was to see everything,
far and near, replied coolly, " Oh, nothing, sir ;
only one of them bloody kings has fallen down
the hatch ! "

In 1821 Commodore Stewart was sent in the
Franklin to the Pacific. The Spanish-American
provinces were struggling for independence
Spain was a friendly Power to whom the United
States owed justice and a strict neutrality. The
" Patriots " possessed all American sympathies.
The Pacific was swarming with buccaneers claiming the protection of Spain, who were depreda-
ting on American commerce, and the " Patriots "
had declared a paper blockade of hundreds of
miles of coast. Stewart owed but one duty, and
that was to his country. He promptly put an
end both to the nominal blockade and to the pro-
tected piracy.

On his return home he was confronted by a
long series of charges, some of trifling, some of
serious import, regarding his demeanor while in
the Pacific. The Navy Department thought best
that these accusations should be submitted to a

court-martial. The court honorably acquitted the commodore, and stated they felt compelled "by a sense of duty to go farther, and to make unhesitatingly this declaration to the world — that, so far from having violated the high duties of neutrality and respect for the laws of nations; so far from having sacrificed the honor of the American flag, or tarnished his own fair fame, by acting upon any motive of a mercenary or sordid kind; so far from having neglected his duty, or betrayed the trust reposed in him by refusing proper protection to American citizens and property, or rendering such protection subservient to individual interests, no one circumstance has been developed throughout the whole course of this minute investigation into the various occurrences of a three years' cruise, calculated to impair the confidence which the members of this court, the navy, and the nation have long reposed in the honor, the talents, and the patriotism of this distinguished officer, or to weaken in any manner the opinion which all who know him entertain of his humanity and disinterestedness. These virtues only glow with brighter lustre from this ordeal of trial, like the stars he triumphantly displayed when valor and skill achieved a new victory to adorn the annals of our naval glory.

Upon the commodore's return from Washington, where his trial took place, to his native city Phil-

adelphia, his friends greeted him with a public
dinner.

Many years later on, his popularity continued
so great that an effort was made to "run" him for
the Presidency. In the course of four months no
less than sixty-seven papers declared for him.
But the project did not receive his sanction; he
gave it no countenance; he would not even discuss it; he was "unusually nervous and fidgety"
during the agitation of the subject; and at length
its promoters were impelled to give it up. He re-
gained his usual equanimity only when his name
ceased to be bandied about by the political press.

Commodore Stewart while on shore was constantly employed upon naval boards and commis-
sions, court-martials, etc., and for many years was
in command of the Philadelphia Navy Yard,
from which latter position he was relieved at his
own request in 1861. He was long the confiden-
tial and trusted adviser of the Navy Department
and the naval committees of Congress. In 1855
Congress created a retiring board, and Stewart
was among its illustrious victims. A few years
afterwards a special Act of Congress was passed,
conferring upon him the title of "Senior Flag Officer" on the active list. He refused to receive
the commission, claiming that he already held that
rank. His commission as Rear Admiral, the first
sent out under the new law, bears date July 16th,
1862.

Admiral Stewart was in his eighty-third year when the insurgents of the South fired upon Fort Sumpter. It roused the blood of the old man's heart to hear of this insult to his nation's flag. At once he wrote to the department imploring to be put on active service. "I am young as ever," he pleaded "to fight for my country." It was hard to deny the old hero the opportunity to draw once more his sword in defence of the flag and Government he loved so well, but younger men were required for the steamship service, to which he was a stranger.

He lived on for nine years more, towards the last suffering fearfully from a deadly disease. In his Life we find this passage : —

" We know how he suffered, and how gradually, yet surely, he was failing. And yet we heard how near the invalid came to blowing himself up in some strange chemical experiment, and what fun he made of the danger. To the last he was cheerful and hopeful — busied with affairs, dictating letters, cracking jokes, expecting soon to be well again. Then he could not leave his bed — was unable to speak without agony — wrote on a slate 'I want'——. They could not read what it was he wanted, his hand trembled so. Perhaps it was the cup of cold water they pressed to his parched lips. Thus, surrounded by those who loved him, the brave spirit passed peacefully away."

" His death took place on the afternoon of November 6th, 1869, he being in the ninety-second year of his age. The council of Bordentown passed appropriate resolutions, the bells tolled their requiem, business was suspended, and the citizens paid their reverence. A government steamer was despatched from the Philadelphia Navy Yard to convey his body to that city. It grounded, and the remains, accompanied by the mayor, council, and distinguished citizens, were conveyed by rail. With the naval escort, the stars shining brightly, they proceeded to Independence Hall, where silently they laid him down, while the old bell tolled forth its solemn notes. The next day, after thousands of citizens had paid their humble reverence, amidst the booming of guns, the muffled notes of bells, and the funeral strains of music, in the presence of the distinguished men of the nation and of the city, and thousands of veterans of the late war for the Union, the old hero's body was given back to mother earth."

His personal appearance, manner, and mental characteristics are described as follows : —

"Commodore Stewart was about five feet nine inches high, and of a dignified and engaging presence. His complexion was fair, his hair chestnut, eyes blue, large, penetrating, and intelligent. The cast of his countenance was Roman, bold, strong, and commanding, and his head finely formed. His control over his passions was truly surprising, and under the most irritating circumstance his oldest seaman never saw a ray of anger flash from his eye. His kindness, benevolence, and humanity were proverbial, but his sense of justice and the requisitions of duty were as unbending as fate. In the moment of greatest stress and danger he was as cool, and quick in judgment, as he was utterly ignorant of fear. His mind was acute and powerful, grasping the greatest or smallest subjects with the intuitive mastery of genius. He was a thorough seaman, and not only fully understood his profession as a naval commander, but all the various interests of commerce, the foreign policy of his country, the principles of government and the law of nations. His numerous official letters and reports, his correspondence and public writings, embracing as they did a wide range of subjects, showed great accuracy of information."

Characteristic of the man are the following anecdote and incident:—

The *Franklin*, while under his command, was lying one night at anchor in Gibraltar Bay, when a sudden blow came up from the eastward, causing her to drag her anchors and go adrift. A midshipman aroused the commander with the startling news: "How's the wind?" said Stewart. "From the east," was the reply; "she has dragged down hill, and is drifting towards Algeria." "Well," was the quiet rejoinder, "the anchors will take when she drifts over there, as it will be up hill on the other side."

"I never lost but one tooth in my life," he said to a friend; "it ached, and I pulled it out with a bullet mould, aboard ship, in a gale of wind."

"As a story-teller Stewart was inimitable; he was famous, moreover, for repartee, and an ever ready wit. His manners were always polite, even distinguished; he dispensed a liberal hospitality, and at the head of his table he was unsurpassed. Throughout he preserved a native dignity, and parried with ease every familiarity, as well as the many inconvenient demands which men in his position are constantly subject to."

On a high bluff of the Delaware, south of Black's Creek, in the environs of Bordentown, is the old country seat of Admiral Stewart, called by him Montpelier, but now generally known as Ironsides. A former proprietor caused to be erected the present large mansion house. The admiral purchased it in 1816, added another story, tastefully laid out the grounds, and planted many white pines, whose tops now reach the height of a hundred feet.

Admiral Stewart left two children, Delia Tudor and Charles Tudor Stewart. Charles graduated at college, became a civil engineer, and assisted in laying out railroads. At twenty-seven years of age he performed so well some delicate work in investigating the affairs of a New Orleans firm engaged in supplying timber for foreign navies that he was taken into partnership, and entrusted with the entire management of the business in Europe. Being well acquainted with Prince Murat, whom he had often befriended during his exile and poverty in Bordentown, the prince presented him to his cousin the Emperor Napoleon the Third, and the chiefs of the Naval Department of France, from whom he obtained heavy contracts for timber. In comparatively a few years he amassed a large fortune. After travelling much through Europe he went to New Orleans, where he studied law and became quite noted in his new profession. He died several years ago, leaving his estate to his sister Delia, who, as has been previously stated, had become the wife of John Henry Parnell.

John Henry and Delia Parnell had five sons and six daughters. Five of the latter and three of the former are still living — namely, John Howard, Charles Stewart, Henry Tudor, the Misses Fanny, Anna, and Theodosia, and two married sisters — Mrs. Thompson, who resides in Paris with her husband; and Mrs. Dickenson, who generally lives in her native land. On the death of their father, at the comparatively early age of forty-eight, he left behind him three estates in Ireland. Charles Stewart Parnell was his fourth son.

Charles' elder brother, John Howard Parnell, inherited a considerable property in the county Armagh, on which he usually resides. He also owns an extensive farm in the State of Alabama. At the general election of 1874 he stood as a Home Rule candidate for the representation of county Wicklow, but was defeated. The remaining and youngest brother, Henry Tudor Parnell, was educated to the bar, and is the owner of landed property in the county Kilkenny. He mostly lives in England. The three unmarried sisters of Mr. C. S. Parnell, as is now pretty generally known, share his Irish sympathies, are proud of the honest manly part he has taken in Irish politics, and are ever ready to defend it and him against all slanderous assailants. They were the first to start subscriptions in America for the Irish people threatened with famine, early in the last quarter of 1879.

Mrs. Delia Parnell, the daughter of Admiral Stewart, brought to her Irish home of Avondale a strong American love of independence, and a hearty hate of British greed and desire for domination. She became in thought and feeling an Irish Nationalist; and from her mainly is derived the warm popular sympathies which glow in the breasts of four of her children. During her residence in Ireland she used the means at her disposal most liberally in alleviating the perennial miseries of the poor around her. At the time of the Fenian troubles she exerted herself in effecting the escape of some who were badly "wanted" by the authorities — a circumstance which procured for her house in Upper Temple Street, Dublin, the distinction of a visit from and search by the police. In the end she retired to the home of her youth, Bordentown, New Jersey, with her unmarried daughters; at which place she spends most of the year, but winters at New York. As the heir of her father and brother, as well as through the resources left her by her husband, she is mistress of an ample income.

Charles Stewart Parnell was born in the month

of June, 1846, at Avondale, Rathdrum, the mansion now in his own possession.

As a child, his mother says, he showed an uncommon love of study; devoting far more time to his books than to the ordinary sports of childhood. His memory was admirable, and he was by no means deficient in wit and sprightliness. As a boy of ten he amused his fellow-passengers in a coach on a country road by comparing the population and military strength of the various countries in Europe, with a view to determining their respective chances in the event of a general war. At this time, however, his mind ran less in the direction of politics than toward mechanical science, and he amused his friends and taxed his own mind not a little in the effort to solve the problem of a perpetual-motion machine. Again, when he wanted some bullets and had no mould in which to form them, he conceived the idea of making them as shot is made — by dropping hot lead from a high tower. The family knew nothing of his design till they were startled by the butler's cry — "Come down there, you young rascal! What are you trying to do?" and the next moment that worthy man rushed up the winding staircase to the roof in time to save the ingenious lad from breaking his neck by a fall of fifty feet to the ground below, where, on the well-worn stones, lay a cake of flattened lead.

Another anecdote of the politician would cause

a moment's wonder that he has not become a military rather than a civil leader of men. The nursery at home was well garrisoned with Liliputian soldiers, of whom Charles commanded one well organized division, while his sister directed the movements of another and opposing force. These never came into actual conflict, but faced one another impassively, while their respective commanders peppered with pop-guns at the enemy's lines. For several days the war continued without apparent advantage being gained by either side. One morning, however, heavy cannonading was heard in the furthest corner of the room (produced by rolling a spiked ball across the floor). Pickets were called in, and in three minutes from the firing of the first shot there was a general engagement all along the line. Strange as it may seem, Miss Parnell's soldiers fell by the score and hundred, while those commanded by her brother refused to waver even when palpably hit. This went on for some time, until, as she obstinately refused to surrender, the young lady's host was completely routed and victory perched upon the standards of her foe. It was learned, from his own confession an hour after this Waterloo, that Charles had, before the battle began, glued his soldiers' feet securely to the table.

Following the un-Irish fashion of his caste — that of the upper classes — John Henry Parnell determined to give his son an English education.

He seems to have been of opinion also that the process 'of Anglicizing could not be too soon begun on the child; for at the age of six little Charles was carried over to and left at a private school near the picturesque little town of Yeovil in Somersetshire. There he remained for about three years. A violent attack of typhoid fever seized him at the Yeovil school, where he lay for weeks at the point of death. His constitution never afterwards quite rallied from the effects of that dreadful prostration; and for years he was considered absolutely a delicate boy. How he has borne up under the accumulated fatigues, exertions, and travels undergone during his active political career seems, when read in the light of the fact last mentioned, but little short of the miraculous.

A couple of years spent amid the bracing airs of the Wicklow hills restored him sufficiently to admit of his being again sent to school. The place selected was again in England — namely, at a spot called Kirk-Langley, near the town of Derby. Here he grew apace, springing up into a tall slender young lad. As the time drew nigh when it was meant that he should enter a university he was placed under the care of the Rev. Mr. Whishaw, then residing at Chipping-Norton, not far from the city of Oxford. This reverend gentleman afterwards became chaplain to the School for the Blind at Liverpool, and enjoys the

reputation of being one of the most celebrated
pulpit orators of that great emporium.

John Henry Parnell had entered the university
of Cambridge himself; and the same university he
selected for his son Charles, who matriculated
there at the age of eighteen. It was the father's
wish that his son should go to the bar; but the
son had no liking for the lawyer's life or work,
and resolutely opposed the parental choice of
a destiny for him. He carried his point, almost
as a matter of course.

He remained but two years at the university,
and so did not graduate. Following in his father's
footsteps, he went abroad to see the world, and
travelled in the United States during the years
1872 and 1873.

As a youth, Charles Stewart Parnell showed no
particular interest in the affairs of Ireland — how
could he with such a denationalizing course of
training as was inflicted on him? — and when he
discussed Irish politics with his sisters he frequently took the Conservative side, to annoy
them in a harmless way. This humor sometimes
worried his mother, who, as she declares, has an
American horror of Toryism. Like his father,
John Henry Parnell, Charles was a skilful crick-
eter, and when at home always took part in the
game, which is much played in Wicklow. In
those days he was something of a wag, and would
keep the table in a roar.

But in the November of 1867 an incident had occurred in Manchester which fastened itself on his memory — the execution of Allen, Larkin, and O'Brien. As he had entered on manhood, and learned to think seriously of men and events, he dwelt on "the Manchester three" and their cruel fate, and thought of the brief, pregnant prayer which came from their lips as they hovered on the dizzy verge of eternity — the immortal "God save Ireland!" At length he resolved to do what in him lay for her safety. He consulted with his uncle Charles Stewart, then living in Paris, and his resolve received the approval of the brave old admiral's son. Next he laid his intention before his mother; and we need hardly observe that Mrs. Delia Parnell was not the one to offer him opposition in such a cause. Finally he took the step of joining the Home Rule League — a decisive one in many ways for him, but especially because it cut him off as a political heretic from several near relatives with whom he would naturally have wished to live in the closest unity, political as well as social.

Having thus thrown in his lot with the people and their supreme cause — the cause of self-government — he was eager to work and make sacrifices in their behalf. The opportunity soon came. Immediately after the general election of 1874, Colonel Taylor, one of the members for Dublin County, having accepted a post in the Govern-

ment, it was needful that he should seek re-
election. The country was then full of spirit and
hope, and it was determined that he should not
have his seat without a fight for it. But a candidate was wanted who would be willing to spend
money freely on the election, for the general good
of the cause, and in the full knowledge that for
the expenditure he must not expect a seat in the
House of Commons.

Charles Stewart Parnell was at hand. He was
asked if he would be the man in the gap on this
occasion, and he willingly consented to take up
the uninviting position of a candidate foredoomed
to defeat.

Though the contest for Dublin County was from
the first a hopeless one on the Home Rule side, it
was, nevertheless, deemed judicious to hold a public meeting in Dublin, in support of Mr. Parnell's
candidature. If such a meeting could attain no
other useful purpose, it would at least introduce
the young and unknown politician to the people
he was so eager to serve. Accordingly, the council of the Home Rule League convened a meeting
in the Rotundo for the afternoon of the 9th of
March, 1874. On the occasion the room was
filled, early as was the hour; the platform was
thronged with an influential and representative
assemblage, including many members of Parliament.

As at this meeting Mr. Parnell made his first

appearance before the public, it is worthy of some
notice in this narrative. Among the M.P.'s present the most prominent were Honest John Martin ;
Isaac Butt, then in reality as well as in name the
trusted leader of the Irish people ; A. M. Sullivan, Mitchell Henry, and Richard O'Shaughnessy.
It was pretty generally known by then that Charles
Stewart Parnell was a scion of the family which
had produced Sir John, the stout and self-sacri-
ficing foe of the Union, and Sir Henry, the life-
long advocate of Catholic equality ; so there was
great enthusiasm among those assembled on that
day in the Rotundo in favor of the relative of
those two worthies who had come forward to
identify himself with the people and their cause.
The popular instinct, which is so seldom wrong in
public affairs, had seized on the fact that the young
man was the inheritor of great reputations and
unsullied memories, and inferred from it that he
would follow in the footsteps of his honored predecessors, and that, in whatever else he might
fail, he might be relied on for honesty of purpose. This was the reason why the room was
thronged at an hour when men in the city are
usually minding their private business, as well as
why so deep an interest was taken in the object of
the meeting.

To Mr. A. M. Sullivan was committed the duty
of proposing the first resolution, which warmly
approved of the candidature of Mr. Charles Stew-

art Parnell.   The speaker had uttered but a few
sentences when there occurred one of those striking
coincidences, dramatic in their effect, which dwell
for ever in the memory of beholders.   Mr. Sullivan was expressing the delight that should be felt,
and the hope that should be inspired, by seeing the
bearers of historic names like that of Parnell
coming back into the ranks of the people; when,
just as the sentence was finished, a tall, slender
young man came through the doorway, and looking neither to the right nor the left, began quietly
making his way through the crowd towards the
platform.   Of those in the room probably not a
score had ever seen him before, nor even heard
his personal appearance described; yet, by some
subtle process of intuition, characteristic of the
Irish mind, it at once became known among the
mass of the large gathering that the new arrival,
so unostentatiously moving up the room, was the
very bearer of a historic name to whom Mr. Sullivan had just referred.   It was like the work of
magic in its wondrous suddenness.   Every eye
was fixed on the young man; people stood on
tiptoe and craned their necks to get a view of
him; while cheer after cheer resounded through
the spacious hall, loud and long-sustained, and
threatening, if not to raise the roof off the place,
at least to split the ears of all in the assembly.
Such a scene of enthusiastic but not disorderly
animation is but rarely witnessed.   Eyes bright-

ened, faces beamed, hats and handkerchiefs waved
in the air, voices were making themselves hoarse;
yet all the while the object of the demonstration,
with bent head and downcast eyes, quietly pursued
his way, as if unconscious of the honor paid him
— or, if conscious, as though he felt it unfitting
to receive popular rewards before he had done
enough to deserve them. Yet it was plain that
his feelings were deeply moved by his reception;
for when he stepped on to the platform he was
pale, and indeed exhibited the appearance of agitation. When, after the last burst of cheering,
Mr. Sullivan, resuming his interrupted speech, confirmed the instinct of the audience by saying that
literally, as well as figuratively, his friend Mr. Parnell had come among them, there was another
enthusiastic outburst, prolonged and deafening;
and before it was over some of the thoughtful
present were asking themselves if a great public
career lay not before this modest-looking youthful
politician, whose very presence, unheralded, un-
announced, could take captive public confidence
in a manner so remarkable. As for the mass,
they waited with impatience for the speech they
expected him to deliver.

The time came for him to speak, and he rose to
his feet to make his first public deliverance, amid
a tempest of cheers. All present saw that he was
laboring under strong emotion, for his color came
and went, and his breast heaved perceptibly.

We can fancy the thoughts which stirred the
fountains of feeling within him to their veriest
depths.   He had resolved to devote himself to his
people, to work for them with all his might; and
here, at the very outset of his career—before, as
it were, he had yet actually put his hand to the
plough — was he receiving an earnest of the gratitude which the Irish people are ever ready to
lavish on all who have even tried honestly to serve
them.   No doubt he knew that the good deeds of
Sir John and Sir Henry Parnell had paved the
way for him to the core of the people's hearts;
and no doubt also he inly resolved at that moment
that he would leave behind him at least the repute
of being as much "a man of integrity" as any one
of his forefathers.   At all events, whatever his
thoughts may have been, he was considerably un-
nerved; for when he began to speak it was in
broken sentences, and in a voice that faltered with
excess of feeling.

It was a scene to be long remembered.   There,
on the front of the platform, by the chairman's
table, he stood, tall, slender, pale, lofty of forehead, his lips unquivering, his chin firm and reso-
lute-looking, his bosom laboring, his brown eyes
flashing over the throng, his back well set up,
and indeed with a carriage that suggested a military training.   And while in the excitement of that
moment—an excitement the exact like of which
he could never again know—his tongue grew un-

willing to express his thoughts, and forced him to
hesitate and to pause, a painfully intent silence
fell on the anxious audience. In the chair was
O'Gorman Mahon, sitting with soldierly erectness
in spite of his advanced years, and with a piercing
gaze fixed on the faltering novice. From the
right of the platform kindly as well as "honest"
John Martin surveyed the young Protestant
patriot, with a benignant smile illuminating his
grave, sweet countenance; the homely, genial face
of Isaac Butt beamed with overflowing good-
nature; the blue eyes of Alexander Sullivan
glowed in eager sympathy, while his whole air in-
dicated to observers an intense desire to spring to
the aid of the speaker, and to invest him with his
own power of apt and fluent expression; Mitchell
Henry, too, from the left of the platform, exhibited an unmistakably kindly interest in the young
speaker, whose native modesty and excited feelings combined to impair his delivery of the
thoughts surging in his brain. Indeed every eye
was riveted on him, both from the platform and
from the floor of the hall; and though a great
many were criticising unfavorably his first effort
as a public speaker, it must be admitted that there
was something in his appearance which impressed
every one favorably, for every one undoubtedly
cheered him without stint.

When the meeting broke up there was a good
deal of discussion among groups of the assem-

blage concerning the chances of the candidate's success in public life. The verdict of many, who had noted only his faltering utterance and his broken sentences, was, " That young man will be a failure. He can't speak." But the shrewder, who had noted the firm set-up of his back and the resolute rigidity of mouth and chin, more sagely observed, "There is *something* in that young man. It will come out in time. Wait and see. " Which section was right all know now.

The Dublin County election at which Mr. Parnell was a candidate is hardly worth referring to further now than to say that, as was expected, he was beaten. It is very well known that the Tories of that county look carefully after the Parliamentary register, year by year; while, on the other hand, hundreds on hundreds of men possessing popular sympathies, and having the needful electoral qualifications, are too apathetic to take the trouble to attend at revision sessions to secure their undoubted right to vote. It must suffice to say that when the polling day had come and gone, and the votes cast had been counted, it was found that Colonel Taylor had received 2,122; that Mr. Parnell's tally was only 1,141; and consequently that the former had been returned by a majority of 981.

One feature of this contested election must still retain a strong interest for every reader. We allude to Mr. Parnell's candidatorial address to the

constituency. Few people have ever dreamt of
referring to it since his defeat; and yet it cannot
but be important to know on what publicly announced principles he began his political career.
They furnish a safe test both of his honesty in
adopting them and his consistency in adhering to
them. We have pleasure, therefore, in reproduc-
ing the main portions of this address, which we are
confident our readers will welcome with equal
pleasure : —

"Upon the great question of Home Rule I will by
all means seek the restoration to Ireland of our domestic Parliament, upon the basis of the resolutions passed
at the National Conference last November, and the
principles of the Home Rule League, of which I am a
member.

"If elected to Parliament I will give my cordial ad-
herence to the resolutions adopted at the recent conference of Irish members, and will act independently
alike of all English parties.

"I will earnestly endeavor to obtain for Ireland a
system of education in all its branches — university,
intermediate, and primary — which will deal impartially with all religious denominations, by affording to
every parent the opportunity of obtaining for his
child an education combined with that religious teach-
ing of which his conscience approves.

"I believe security for his tenure, and the fruits of
his industry, to be equally necessary to do justice to
the tenant and to promote the prosperity of the whole
community. I will, therefore, support such an exten-

sion of the ancient and historic tenant-right of Ulster, in all its integrity, to the other parts of Ireland, as will secure to the tenant continuous occupation at fair rents."

In addition he promised to work for "a complete and unconditional amnesty;" and, after a graceful reference to the efforts made by his relatives, Sir John and Sir Henry, for the good of the Irish people, he concluded:—

"If you elect me I will endeavor, and think I can promise, that no act of mine will ever discredit the name which has been associated with these recollections."

No need to ask now whether any act of his has since discredited that name. Has he fulfilled both in letter and spirit those early pledges given when a young untried man? Has he sought the restoration of our domestic Parliament "by all means"? Has he acted "independently alike of all English parties"? Has he been idle in reference to the land question? Was he "behind the door" in regard to the amnesty? Has he neglected the cause of religious equality in education? Most of our readers remember enough of the political life of the last five years to give to all of these questions such answers as could not fail to be complimentary to Mr. Charles Stewart Parnell. Yet in the rush and hurry of the time people forget many things which are worth recol-

lection; and we purpose in this narrative to
recall several such things to their memories —
events of deep interest and great importance to
the Irish nation.

After the Dublin election nothing was heard by
the public of Mr. Parnell till John Mitchel came
over from America, after his long exile, to beard
the British lion in his den by seeking the representation of Tipperary County. Two circumstances in connection with that event roused
Charles Parnell to active sympathy on the rebel
candidate's behalf. One was the opportunity
given of striking a resounding blow against British domination in Ireland; the other was the in-
domitable, unconquerable spirit of Mitchel himself,
so near akin to Mr. Parnell's own. On this occasion he emerged from the privacy into which he
had retired after the Dublin County election, in
an admirably written letter to the papers, announcing his hearty approbation of Mitchel's
course, and giving £25 towards the expenses of
the contest which Mr. Stephen Moore of Barna
forced on "the premier county."

Tipperary put Mitchel at the head of the poll by
an immense majority, but he died, alas! in the
arms of victory. At his funeral his brother-in-
law, political colleague, and fellow-convict, John
Martin, was seized with a mortal illness, and
within a week followed him to the grave. John
Martin's death took place the 29th of March, 1875.

Ireland was stricken with sorrow; but Meath
County bewailed a special loss, for in gentle John
Martin she had had a representative as honest and
earnest, as upright and firm, as ever championed
the cause of "Ireland a nation" in the London
House of Commons. To find a fitting successor
for such a man was no easy task; but by a happy
stroke of fortune Charles Stewart Parnell, having
been recommended by the council of the Home
Rule League, was adopted as the popular candidate by a large representative meeting of the
electorate. Another Home Ruler, a solicitor of
much local influence, opposed him; and a Tory
gentleman of the county, beholding a prospect of
division in the national ranks, and fancying that
he might be able to slip into the seat through the
split, also took the field. When, on the 19th of
April, 1875, the votes having been counted, the
declaration of the poll was made, it was found
that the numbers were — Charles Stewart Parnell,
Home Ruler, 1,771; J. L. Naper, Tory, 902; J.
T. Hinds, Home Ruler, 138; from which figures
it will be seen that the mass of the electors refused
to play the game of the common enemy by fighting among themselves.

There was tremendous rejoicing in Royal Meath
over the victory. Enthusiastic crowds assembled
in thousands to give vent to a common feeling of
delight; bonfires blazed in many quarters; and
the populace of Trim, in which town the declara-

tion of the poll had been made, having discovered Mr. Parnell walking down from the parochial house to his hotel, laid lovingly violent hands on him, carried him in triumph round their own special bonfire in the market square, and finally set him standing on the head of a cask to speak a few words to them. To those acquainted with the Irish nature it is unnecessary to say that no such wild familiarity would have been taken with him if during the course of his canvass he had not become a popular favorite.

Mr. Parnell did not delay to receive congratulations on his success. Parliament was in session at the period of his election, and, moreover, the Government had just then in hands a Coercion Bill for Ireland. Mr. Joseph Gillis Biggar had determined that this proposed tyrannical enactment should be met with a stiff resistance. Therefore the new member for Meath, who meant work, not pleasure, hurried over to London, formally took his seat, and was in good time to record his first vote against the Coercion Bill on the 22d of April, 1875. As he was in Trim on the night of the 19th, it is plain that he "did not let the grass grow under his feet," to use an expressive Irish phrase.

The struggle over the Coercion Bill was stout and prolonged. Mr. Biggar began it with the famous four hours' speech which drove the assembled Commons at Westminster into alternate flushes of rage and despair. That struggle was the first taste they had got of what has since been called "Obstruction"—a word which merely expresses briefly that it is within the power of even a few resolute Irish members of Parliament to prevent any administration from having everything its own way. That struggle further showed that even a score of resolute Irish members could at least prevent anything approaching to bad measures for their country. It remained for Mr. Parnell afterwards to prove that good measures could also be obtained by a continued pursuance of the same method.

Only on the 11th of April did the bill get through the House of Commons, after a consumption of Government time which caused in Great Britain a feeling of positive dismay. There were, of course, a large number of divisions over the various amendments proposed; and it is to be recorded to the credit of Charles Stewart Parnell that, even at the very outset of his Parliamentary career, he was present and took the Irish side, in every one of those divisions. Others there were of his colleagues, much more advanced in years, infinitely better known to the public, and possessing the full confidence of too confiding constituencies, who were absent again and again with no better cause than a desire to take their pleasure in London drawing-rooms. But he stood up to his work with a diligence from which they might have taken example. The rest of the session passed over without anything remarkable being done by "the Irish party" in Parliament; and during that period Mr. Parnell was by far more constant in his attendance than the majority of his fellow-members. He did not address the House; but employed himself much in mastering its cumbrous and intricate forms and the rules which guide its course of procedure.

Now there was a representative of Cork city, who, having been a hot revolutionist in '48, had taken refuge under the stars and stripes, and dwelt in America for many years, in the practice of his profession of civil engineer. Having amassed a fortune, he returned to his native land, and set up his habitation on the banks of the beautiful Lee. He had profited by contact with the shrewd American mind; and when he had observed the London Commons for some time he came to a conclusion which he expressed in pretty much the following fashion : —

" You will never get them to listen to you until you begin to take as active an interest in English affairs as they take in Irish ones. I am too old to have the necessary energy for the work. Why don't some of you young fellows try it ? "

The man who said this was generally spoken of with affectionate familiarity as "Honest Joe Ronayne." Peace to his ashes ! He died in the

Spring of 1876. He loved Ireland well, and
served her well too, and will be long borne in
her grateful memory.

Charles Parnell heard the saying, and pondered
deeply on it. The more he thought of it the
more it appeared like a revelation; until at
length he determined that, since the practised
speakers among the Irish members seemed to
shrink from the labor involved, he himself would
test the wisdom of Joe Ronayne's dictum. With
this view he set himself to looking out for some
Government measure in which he could take a
tremendous interest. He eventually chose the
English Prisons Bill, which proposed to hand
over the management of local prisons to the ex-
ecutive; and he made the selection with a view
to first modifying it to his desires, and afterwards
insisting that the Irish Prisons Bill which was to
follow should be modelled on the precedent thus
afforded. For it occurred to Mr. Parnell that
the time of political prosecutions in Ireland had
not yet passed away, and that it would be wise
to prepare for occurrences of the kind, to the
extent at least of saving those convicted of sedition from the indignities and maltreatment to
which theretofore they had been invariably subjected in Irish jails.   .

We have previously intimated that Mr. Parnell
had little or no experience in public speaking.
From native modesty, or a diffidence in his own

powers, he shrank from obtruding himself on audiences accustomed to being addressed by orators, rhetoricians, and practised debaters. But to carry out the scheme of tactics which was slowly maturing in his mind it was absolutely needful to gain such experience; and to the task he began to set himself at the beginning of the Parliamentary session of 1876. The strength of his purpose impelled him to surmount every obstacle that lay in his path; so he made use of the House of Commons as a debating society in which he might acquire ease and fluency of public address.

The first opportunity of which he took advantage was of a kind peculiarly grateful to him. It was supplied by the very first of the resolute struggles to which some members of the Irish Parliamentary party have since very often treated the assembled Commons of Westminster, and which have received from the newspapers the expressive designation "scenes in the House."

The "scene" to which reference is now made arose in this way. Early in each session the Commons elect members to sit on various committees having certain duties to discharge in connection with the business of the House. The Whig and Tory party leaders usually agreed beforehand on a list of members for each committee, taken impartially from the ranks of both parties in fair proportion to their respective

numbers; with the result that when the elections
came on each name was passed simply as a matter
of course — such a thing as taking a division
against any one being almost unheard of. The
formation of a third party — the Home Rule one
— disturbed the little arrangement mentioned;
and at the beginning of 1876 both Whigs and
Tories combined totally to ignore the existence of
that third party by drawing no members of committees from its ranks. Some of the Irish representatives made up their minds to resent this
grossly unfair course of the English party mana-
gers by indiscriminately challenging every name
put up for election.

Late on the night of Monday, the 6th of March,
there being at the time but six members of the
Irish party present — of whom, as might be expected, the ever-diligent Charles Stewart Parnell
was one — a motion was made " That the select
committee on referees on private bills do consist
of twenty-one members." Absurdly few as were
the Home Rulers on the spot, they determined to
fight the matter out with resolution, and to teach
the Whig and Tory conspirators a lesson they
would not soon forget. Mr. A. M. Sullivan
promptly rose to his feet, and moved that the
number of the committee should be twenty-three
instead of twenty-one, with the object of adding
on two of his own party. The gage of battle
thus thrown down was quickly taken up by the

overwhelming majority furnished from the ranks
of the two British parties, united for the occasion,
as usual, in doing an injustice to the Irish.   They
won in the division of course, although on the
Irish side there voted several fair-minded Englishmen — there *are* fair-minded Englishmen even in
the London House of Commons — whose aid
brought the Irish muster up to twenty-one.

Immediately "the scene" began.   Every name
put up was challenged in turn, and a division
taken on it.   What that meant, and how great was
the loss of time it involved, will be understood
when we say that previous to each division two
minutes are allowed before the closing of the entrance door of the House, to allow of members
rushing in from the bar, the dining-room, the
smoke-room, the library, and so forth, to take
part in the division, although they may not have
the faintest idea of what it is about.   The members are warned of each division by the ringing of
bells set up for the purpose.   When the door is
closed, the Commons file slowly into two great
corridors known as "the division lobbies," one devoted to the "ayes" and the other to the "noes."
In the entrance to these lobbies stand the respective "tellers," who stop each member as he
passes, and take down his name.   When the names
are all entered, they are very carefully counted,
all return to the chamber where sits Mr. Speaker,
and the numbers for and against are announced.

There is usually some cheering after each announcement; and when that is over the House proceeds again to business. Each division ordinarily takes about fifteen minutes.

From the above it will easily be seen that if a number of divisions be taken in a night, not only is "the time of the House" consumed but a good deal of enforced pedestrianism falls to the lot of members, many of whom from one cause or other may not be very well able to walk, especially in the small hours of the morning. And it was precisely to such consumption of time and such enforced pedestrianism the resolute Irish six condemned their unscrupulous Whig and Tory opponents. Naturally these latter became annoyed under the punishment they were receiving, and a good deal of temper was displayed. It is in the midst of one of the short but warm discussions of the night that we find the first record of Mr. Parnell addressing his fellow Commoners. The hour was one at which Parliamentary reporters do not trouble themselves to take down the sayings of members in full, therefore the record is extremely brief; but one phrase of it is so characteristic of Mr. Parnell that there is hardly room for doubt that it was reported in the exact words which fell from his lips. The report goes: —

"Mr. Parnell said they had deliberately adopted this course, and *they would stick to it.*"

Significant words indeed, if his hearers but knew their full meaning when coming from him. And stick to it he did. Respect for not a name on the list was shown. Division followed division with a regularity beyond all praise. The weary Britishers walked in and out of their lobby muttering execrations on the heads of those obstinate Irish who still kept up the battle, and would not acknowledge themselves vanquished. The counting of British noses was a toilsome process, there were so many of them. On the Irish side the counting was easy indeed, for their English allies fell away after the first division, and the Home Rule tellers had only five names to put down; after the twelfth the number fell to three.

A compromise was suggested; but the Britishers, who would have been glad to agree to it an hour earlier, were now thoroughly irate; in defiance of Dr. Watts, they had "let their angry passions rise;" and with their tremendous majority they were resolved not to give way an inch. Appeals were made to the Irish to cease a hopeless struggle; and then, we read in the report:—

"Mr. Parnell said the compromise had been refused, and the fight should go on."

And on it went steadily; the Irish cool but determined, the Britishers wild with rage, and now and again giving angry vent to their excited feelings. The gallant Major O'Gorman led his di-

vision of three into the lobby, having called on
the honorable member for Meath to be his co-teller.
The honorable member for Meath gladly obliged his
honorable and gallant friend.   The thirteenth division was taken, and still the fight was not at an end.
The fourteenth followed, and then the fifteenth ;
and when, at a quarter past four in the morning,
the result of the sixteenth was announced, the an-
griest Whig or Tory of them all had been brought
to his senses.   Though the names proposed were
every one carried, and in that sense the Britishers
might congratulate themselves on winning several
petty successes, yet the end for which the few Irish
struggled was achieved—the exclusion of members of their party had to be given up—the attempt to ignore the existence of a distinct third
party in the House was defeated—and in that
sense, the true one, victory was with the Irish,
their operations had been successful, and they had
conquered all along the line.

It was during this session of 1876 that Mr.
Parnell began to cultivate that devotion to the
Governmental estimates for which he afterwards
became so distinguished.   There were many "great
debates " got up that year by the Home Rule party
— field-day displays which gave the do-nothings
an opportunity of posing before their constituents
as zealous servants, through the easy means of
letting off in the House elaborate speeches to which
no one paid any attention during their deliverance,

but which were pretty certain to find their way
into the columns of the Irish press, and to receive
therein an amount of space which gave them a
solid, substantial, responsible look, calculated to
impress the minds of admiring but extremely
simple electors to the West of St. George's Chan-
nel. Of course we are not to be understood as
attributing no value whatever to such debates.
On the contrary, they have their use, and are indeed at times necessary. But if there ends the
work of Irish members in the English Parliament
the advantage of the field-days is small indeed.
Mr. Parnell allowed any one who chose to take a
prominent part in those displays. For himself he
did not care for them. He saw that hypocrites
systematically made use of them for the purpose
of throwing dust in the eyes of their constituencies, so he merely closed his lips more tightly,
and waited with what patience he might for the
crushing defeat sure to follow on the division —
for which, however, he took care to be on hand.
But he did active work when the House went into
committee, and contrived to make himself, by sheer
practice, an excellent debater. And when he felt
the needful confidence in himself he proposed on
his own responsibility a motion in favor of the
political prisoners, which he supported in a telling
speech, powerful not only in argument but in the
unusual boldness of the tone which struck the
ears of the British Commons. The date of this

effort to redeem the pledge regarding amnesty, given in his earliest address as a Parliamentary candidate, was the 22nd of May, 1876.

In his speech on this occasion — which may be regarded as his first sustained effort at speech-making — he made such references to the trials consequent on the rescue of Kelly and Deasy from the police van at Manchester as startled most of his hearers. One of them, Sir Michael Hicks-Beach, then Chief Secretary for Ireland, bore Mr. Parnell's remarks bitterly in mind; and when, in the Home Rule debate on the 30th June, the torpid English baronet rose to speak against the Irish claim, he lugged in by the horns, as it were, a direct allusion to what Mr. Parnell had said on the 22nd of May previously. This proceeding of Secretary Beach was a distinct breach of a rule of the London House of Commons which prohibits members from referring to any previous debate of the same session; yet, singular to relate, he was not called to order by any authority of the assembly. However, Sir Michael of the retentive memory but little knew at that time the kind of man whom he had singled out for a thrust. He, as well as every one of his colleagues, is better informed by now, and none, we fancy, would go out of his way to assail the honorable member for Meath. Even at that time the baronet was not allowed to remain long undeceived; for Mr. Parnell rose

to his feet on the instant, interrupted Sir Michael,
and calmly retorted as follows : —

"The right honorable gentleman looked at me so
directly when he said he regretted that any member of
this House should apologize for murder, that I wish to
say, as publicly and directly as I can, that I do not
believe, and never shall, that any murder was committed at Manchester."

It will be remembered that it was the fate of the
Manchester Three which first set Mr. Parnell
thinking seriously of Ireland and her unhappy
destinies ; and at no time since has he been prepared to listen silently to any defamation concerning them. The imprudent Secretary, on hearing
the observation quoted above, seemed for a while
like one who had received a good box on the ear ;
he stammered out a Parliamentary paraphrase of
"I didn't know you'd take it that way, I'm sure ;"
and then, carefully avoiding any further allusion
to either the Manchester cases or the honorable
member for Meath, addressed himself to his subject proper.

One other feature of Mr. Parnell's conduct during this session of 1876 deserves notice here. He
attended strictly to party discipline. Whenever
there were meetings of the Irish party he was
present ; whatever the decision arrived at by the
majority he helped to carry it out. Nay, on
occasions — and there was at least one — when
Mr. Butt earnestly wished his followers to abstain

altogether from voting on Imperial questions, so
as to preserve intact the individuality of the party,
and to exhibit its strength conspicuously to both
Whigs and Tories ; and when men like MacCarthy,
Downing and Major O'Gorman obstinately refused
to be led by their leader, and insisted on their
right to vote with the English party of their
choice ; Mr. Parnell was one of the small faithful
band who followed Mr. Butt in a body out of the
chamber when the bells for the division were set
a-ringing ; as, for instance, after the debate on the
proclamation giving to Queen Victoria the title of
Empress of India — a debate which came off on
the 11th of May, 1876.

Yet at the very time that Mr. Parnell, for the
sake of union, submitted so willingly to the bonds
of party discipline, and obeyed with such alacrity
the wishes expressed by the party leader, he was
conscious that all was not well in that organization, and he had already begun a kind of guerilla
warfare against the House of Commons, in conjunction with his stanch friend and ally, sturdy
Joseph Biggar, one of the members for Cavan.
He was also projecting a sterner struggle for the
next session.   He had mastered the " rules of the
House ;" he had had practice in debate, both in
Parliament and in the consulting rooms of the
Irish party ; his diffidence had been torn away in
the conflicts wherein he had engaged ; self-con-
sciousness had been driven off, and in its stead

there remained only the rapidly growing power of
his unflinching purpose.   His laborious attendance in Parliament for several consecutive months
compelled a brief rest for a couple of weeks in
June ; but he was back in his place in time for the
Land Bill and for. the Home Rule debate in which
he so bewildered Sir Michael Hicks-Beach towards the end of that month.

So far he was comparatively unknown to the
general Irish public ; but keen observers of political events had noted his course ; and when, in the
August of 1876, the Home Rule Confederation of
Great Britain, to test the practical value of the
Irish Convention Act, since repealed, determined
to hold their annual convention in Dublin, it
was Mr. Charles Stewart Parnell who was put
into the second chair at their public meeting
in the evening, when the vote of thanks was proposed to Isaac Butt for presiding, although there
were several other members of Parliament present,
whose age and acknowledged standing in the
political world were much beyond Mr. Parnell's.

During the Winter of 1866-7 he reflected much
on Joe Ronayne's pithy saying, and gradually improved his plan of operations against the anti-
Irish majority in the London House of Commons.
While still adhering to his intention to take an
active interest in purely English affairs, he saw
his way also to working successfully for the benefit of Irish ones.   Since the formation of the Irish

party a sessional "rule of the House" had been framed to prevent measures from going forward a stage after half-past twelve at night if notice of opposition of any kind had been formally given. It seemed to be a most innocent rule — a rule devised to let members go off home to bed at some approach to reputable hours — a rule, in fact, with which no respectable man, be he member of Parliament or not, côuld quarrel.   As a matter of fact, however, it was employed to stay the passage of the various bills brought in by the Irish party; notice of opposition having been promptly given to every one of them, while other bills of all kinds remained unopposed.   The rule had been found to work so well in the way intended that it was again triumphantly passed at the opening of the session of 1877.   Forthwith Mr. Parnell and Mr. Biggar indiscriminately gave formal notice of opposition to a score of English and Imperial bills, by which simple tactical proceeding they brought them all under the operation of the half-past twelve rule, and so checkmated the wily British schemers.   The cry of "obstruction" was at once raised by those injured innocents; vague but dreadful punishments on the offending pair were darkly menaced in the British prints; cold looks from the majority of their own colleagues, and angry ones from the great mass of British members, met Messrs. Parnell and Biggar for their spirited but most natural action; everything was done by friend and foe alike to make their position most unpleasant; yet, though they did not revel, as Mark Tapley might have done, in the annoyances that incessantly met them—indeed, if the plain truth is to be told, they felt the bolts keenly enough when shot by their own colleagues —they held persistently in the course on which they had entered, and dug a deep grave for that "rule of the House" which had been so craftily utilized to hamper the bills brought in by the Irish party.

It is quite possible—nay, even probable—that there are many people who believe that Mr. Parnell's zeal in the cause of Irish peasant-proprietorship is a new thing—that the idea is one he suddenly adopted merely to gain access of popularity—that, in short, he had no real conviction on the question when early in 1879 he began to advocate it so strenuously. Well, to such doubters of his good faith in the matter we commend the fact that on the 14th of February, 1877, he urged the British House of Commons to assent to the second reading of a bill whose provisions were wholly directed towards making more easy the conversion of tenant-farmers into peasant-proprietors. The title of the bill was "The Irish Church Act Amendment Bill;" and its sole object was to amend the Church Disestablishment Act in such a way that those tenants who held the glebe lands should have much greater facilities

and inducements for becoming owners than the
Act originally afforded. His able statement converted a great many British members to his views.
In the division 110 followed him into the lobby,
of whom but 39 were his party colleagues. Only
150 in all voted against his bill. Though he did
not win a complete victory over British prejudice,
he helped very materially to bring the principle of
Irish peasant-proprietorship to the front; and in
any case he then put beyond question the good
faith of his subsequent advocacy of that solution
of the Irish land problem.

Before reverting to Mr. Parnell's Parliamentary
career in 1877 — which was a most notable one
indeed — we must refer, however briefly, to a very
interesting event in which he figured prominently,
and which could not but have had some effect, not
only on the results of his American mission in
1879, but also in deepening and widening the
kindly relations between Ireland and the United
States. In the Autumn of 1876 the project was
mooted of sending from the Irish people a con-
gratulatory address to the States on the centenary
of their independence. It was known in Ireland
that the people of the Union meant to celebrate
that glorious hundredth anniversary with unparalleled displays of public rejoicing; and with
those rejoicings the Irish, so long suffering from
the loss of their own independence, could more
than any other people in Europe keenly sympa-

thize. It was resolved to put that sympathy in evidence in a form that would endure. No sooner was the project mooted in the press than its promoters found it so warmly and widely taken up that they conceived they had absolutely national sanction for the undertaking. An enormous mass meeting of the citizens of the Irish metropolis adopted the address "from the Irish nation," which was inscribed to President Grant as the chief representative of the Union. Messrs. Parnell and O'Connor Power were deputed as the bearers of this historical document, which was richly illuminated on parchment and splendidly framed.

The two gentlemen proceeded on their mission towards the close of 1876. Arrived at their destination they found themselves confronted by obstacles which hindered them from fulfilling the trust confided to them. President Grant declined to receive the address from its bearers. If he should accept it at all on behalf of the American people it should come through the British ambassador at Washington. It was roundly asserted at the time that the said ambassador had himself raised this difficulty for the two Irish envoys. However that may be, Messrs. Parnell and Power could see nothing but a wild incongruity in presenting through a British ambassador an address congratulating a people on having been fortunate enough to fling off the British yoke, and coming from a people who were themselves struggling to get rid of British domination. The President stood firm in the position he had taken up. The two Irishmen would on no account agree to the condition he imposed; and to ordinary observers it seemed as if the mission must turn out a conspicuous failure.

But those who knew something of Mr. Parnell's energy and readiness of resource did not believe he would be so easily baffled; nor were they mistaken. Cancelling the illuminated parchment brought from Dublin, he got another illuminated, paying for it from his own purse; and in this copy of the address he substituted for the superscription to President Grant one to the people of the States. This he determined to have accepted, if possible, by the House of Representatives at Washington. In the end his change of tactics proved eminently successful; although, being anxious to prove his new scheme of policy against the tyrant majority in the British House of Commons, he recrossed the Atlantic before the reception of the address by Congress.

The session of 1877 was the most memorable for extraordinary scenes in British Parliamentary history. Beginning with the opposition of Messrs. Parnell and Biggar to " the half-past twelve rule," and concluding with the famous twenty-two hours' debate on the South African Bill, there occurred a succession of unexampled episodes, in every one

of which Mr. Parnell was a prominent figure. It
was from no love of notoriety that the energetic
member for Meath took such a conspicuous part
in those unusual proceedings. We have already
said that he knew that all was not well with the
Home Rule party. The utter indifference to the
interests of their country, displayed by the majority of them, was a perpetual goad to him. Other
members of the party also had been galled by that
indifference — Mr. Biggar notably so. Mr. A. M.
Sullivan had commented on it in the press as delicately as he might, only with the effect of evoking
a tumult against himself from those whose con-
sciences pointed them out as culprits. · Even Mr.
Butt, although he totally disapproved of the new
tactics inaugurated by Messrs. Parnell and Biggar,
was yet most painfully aware of the want of earnestness and genuineness of too many of his followers. In private he often spoke bitterly about
the discouraging fact; and once at least he gave
vent to his feelings in public. At a banquet given
to him in Dublin in the first week of February,
1877, he alluded, in the course of a magnificent
speech, to the remissness of the majority of the
party, in terms which it must prove interesting to
the reader to have now recalled. He said :—

"I hope that during the ensuing session we shall
have a full attendance of Irish members — such an
attendance as shall enable us to act effectively in the
small hours of the morning, when discussing in Parlia-

ment the questions in which we are so interested. It is not in great parades the battle of Ireland is to be fought. The man does not serve Ireland who comes over only two or three times in the session. The cause is not served by such a man, even though he take the opportunity of making a grand speech. Many men have done far wiser in making no speeches at all, but who have been always present at the hour of need — present at any hour of the morning when their services were of material use to the cause of their country. Now I do think I have a right to ask the attention of the Irish people. Give me whole-hearted support — give me whole-hearted support — no half-hearted support — or rather, if you will, infuse into half-hearted supporters the whole of your own support; and then when the day does come, when the struggle is passed, when future generations will pronounce their judgment on the part acted by an individual so humble as myself — and believe me that the man placed in the position you place me in will occupy a place in the historic page — let me be judged fairly. If I struggle, let the Irish people struggle too, and then I will not be ashamed or look with fear to the place that my name will occupy."

Here positively we have Mr. Parnell's views powerfully expressed ; and we only can say now it was a pity that Mr. Butt, starting with the same ideas, should have veered so wide apart from his young follower in the conclusions he ultimately reached. As for Mr. Butt's appeal for whole-hearted support from the do-nothings of the party, so far as its effect on them was concerned, it might as well have been addressed to the bricks in the walls of the room in which his speech was delivered. His sentiments were cheered to the echo; nevertheless the majority of the party remained as reluctant as ever to act up to them.

Under the circumstances so referred to by the leader of the party Mr. Parnell felt himself thoroughly justified in following his own course for the benefit of Irish interests, and especially of the cause of self-government, whether with or without the approval of Mr. Butt. That able and distinguished man, astute as he was in most affairs, was yet unable to perceive the exact bearing of the new policy. He regarded it as plain and simple obstruction of the business of the House of Commons, and again and again prophesied that it would be put down. But Mr. Parnell had no notion of taking up an attitude which he could not maintain; and one of the cardinal features of the novel plan of action he had struck out — one, too, which seems wholly to have escaped Mr. Butt's notice — was to endeavor to benefit the British democracy while offering steady opposition to a British aristocratic Government. By this simple means he at once served the broad interests of humanity, incapacitated the London Parliament for speedy work, and provided an excellent and sure-acting buffer which saved himself from being crushed.

On this principle he stood while opposing the English Prisons Bill, to which embryo piece of legislation he had given very close study. All his amendments (and he proposed a great many indeed) were directed towards liberalizing the measure. He wanted to secure even criminals from brutal treatment inside the prison walls, and from being compelled by the cruelty of jailors to suffer punishments beyond those to which they had been condemned ; he wanted adequate supervision and inspection of prisons ; he wanted, above all, to save political prisoners from the degradations properly meted out in jail to the murderous burglar, the callous baby-farmer, or the beast convicted of unspeakable crimes. Amendment after amendment was proposed by him only to be lost ; and still on succeeding clauses of the bill he calmly brought up fresh amendments having in view the same or similar objects. The bill, in consequence, made little or no headway in committee ; and the wrath of the hitherto omnipotent majority steadily accumulated against the daring offender who by his audacious pertinacity was single-handed proving himself a match for hundreds.

And just now Mr. Parnell developed a singular zeal in the interests of the soldiers of Great Britain, and devoted himself with heroic constancy to the improvement of their lot by moving amendments to the Mutiny Bill—a measure which had been therefore passed annually as a mere matter of form, and any provision of which the ordinary British member would have deemed it sacrilege to touch.

The gathering waters of rage in the end burst through the dam, and there came "a scene in the House." It was immediately after the Easter recess; the hour was advanced in the morning; Mr. Parnell had been at constant and harassing work for some ten hours; he wished to propose some new amendments on a clause about to be discussed, and, as he had not the amendments prepared, and was besides completely worn out, he made the quite reasonable suggestion that the committee should postpone its further labors to another date.

Let the reader picture to himself the scene which followed. The London House of Commons is eighty feet long by fifty wide, and is forty feet in height. The entrance door is at the foot of this spacious apartment; and, facing the door, at the head of the room, is the Speaker's chair. A T-shaped table stands in front of the Speaker's chair. Either side of the table rise up seats, tier on tier, the higher each about twelve inches above the one next below, and all lying lengthwise down the room. Scattered over those seats are some hundred members of Parliament, most of them in the regulation "full dress" of London — white tie, much shirt-front, small black waistcoat, black trousers, and black swallow-tail

coat. Many of these gentlemen have just come
to the House from dinner-parties at which wine
has been flowing pretty freely ; others have looked
in on their way home from balls where copious
libations of champagne had been offered up to
pleasure. These are boisterous. On the front
bench to the right of the Speaker's chair are half
a dozen members of the Government, asleep or
pretending to be asleep. In the chair sits the
chairman of committees, flushed and angry-look-
ing — his face suggestive of a wish to have some
one laid under a Nasmyth steam-hammer in full
blast. Far down the room, to the left of the
chair, stands erect a slim young man, calm, composed, gentlemanly, undemonstrative either in
voice or gesture, and he is striving to address
the House. The convivial gentlemen converse
quite loudly with each other, and in concert, as if
of set purpose ; and the voice of the speaker is
smothered in the noise. The chairman does not
interfere. The young man persists, and raises
his voice above the din, which suddenly grows
twice as great as before. The speaker's pale face
waxes paler still, and there is an ominously bright
sparkle in his brown eyes ; further than this there
is no sign that he is moved by the vulgar rude-
ness which assails him. He pauses, standing still
erect. There comes a lull in the designed confusion ; and into that lull he interjects a sharp, clear,
terse sentence, not at all conveying compliments

to the House. Then the hilarious young gentlemen of from thirty-four to forty who have been
out dancing, or dining and wining, begin to dis-
play the variety of their accomplishments. Three
or four, as if to emphasize that frugality of nature's gifts to them which, among their acquaint-
ances, causes them to be set down as "asses,"
begin to bray. Others mimic the cries of barn-
yard fowl with more or less success. Some
whistle as if they were lunatics who fancied themselves railway locomotives giving out a warning;
some ironically shriek "yaw-yaw"—which is
English for "hear, hear"; others scream "'vide,
'vide"—English for "divide, divide"; and one,
a sprig of nobility, very accurately reproduces
the sounds made by a man whose stomach revolts
against the inordinate quantity of strong liquor
with which he has overladen it.

Calmly, in spite of all, the speaker goes on
whenever a moment's lull gives him a chance.
He talks as argumentatively as though he were
addressing a roomful of philosophers, and he does
not resume his seat until he has finished the reasons
which impel him to move "that the chairman do
report progress"—one of the forms for bringing
to an end a sitting of the House in committee.

And now occurs a regrettable incident. Mr.
Butt has been taking his ease outside in one of
the lobbies. Mr. Butt is genial to a fault; he is
impressionable too; he is not fond of fighting at

all; he has a cordial dislike of wounding British susceptibilities; and, to crown all, in the words which Major O'Gorman once applied to him during his lifetime at a public meeting, "He is too soft with those English — he often says 'hear, hear,' when he should say 'no, no.'" Some one rushes out of the House to seek Mr. Butt, finds him, gives him a garbled account of what had been taking place inside, and induces him to come in and use his influence in putting down the terrible young man who not only stops the wheels of the Parliamentary machine, and threatens to smash it up altogether, but is also "doing incalculable damage to the Home Rule cause." How tender the regard of Englishmen just then for "the Home Rule cause!"

Mr. Butt, without thinking, and without taking the trouble to make sure that his informant had not deceived him, launches out into a denunciation of Mr. Parnell which earns for the denouncer the hearty cheers of the assembly, the aforesaid convivial young men verging on middle age included. There is great smiling in the British ranks at this episode, and much mutual congratulation. Surely Mr. Parnell will hearken to the voice of his leader; surely he is now effectually muzzled and fettered; surely they can get through their Mutiny Bill that night, and so put it beyond the power of any Irish member thereafter to busy himself in a matter so purely and entirely English.

These were "the pleasing hopes, the fond desires," in which British members indulged as Mr.
Butt poured out with rapid tongue his heated ut-
terances ; and it does not seem to have occurred
to any one of those members that an Irish member's right to take an active part in the settlement
of purely English affairs has been, since the
Union, quite as good as an English member's to
take an active part in purely Irish affairs ; though
the latter occurs frequently every session.

But alas for those delightful speculations ! Mr.
Parnell, though grieved at the tone taken up by
Mr. Butt, was not to be turned aside from his
purpose. As it is the privilege of any member to
move alternately the motions, " That the chairman
do report progress," and "That the chairman do
leave the chair," just so long as he chooses, it
came to pass, the moment it was found that Mr.
Parnell had really made up his mind to have the
further consideration of the Bill postponed, that
the House and the Government gave way, seeing
plainly that nothing whatever was to be gained by
a continuance of the fight, and that nothing could
result from it but increased disorder and confusion.
They had had some experience of Mr. Parnell by
that time, and they had already learned that when
he entered deliberately on any course he would
" stick to it." The Bill was therefore held over to
another date.

The wear and tear of struggling almost single-hand against hundreds, as well as of his close and constant attendance in the House the whole time it remained sitting, began even so early in the session to tell on Mr. Parnell's health. Instead of prescribing for himself a period of rest, he sent over to Ireland for a couple of his hunters, on which he could every day take a spin in the fresh rural air, and so brace himself up physically for the hard work still before him.

Meanwhile Mr. Butt had thought proper privately to lecture Messrs. Parnell and Biggar on what he thought the folly of their course. He was annoyed with the majority of his followers for doing nothing; but he was still more annoyed with a small minority for doing what he considered too much. The members for Meath and Cavan, however, while responding courteously, declined to have their hands tied by their leader on matters outside his jurisdiction. The leader appealed to the party; and as the earnestness and activity of Messrs. Parnell and Biggar was in itself an incessant and stinging reproach to the majority for their total want of either one quality or the other, the majority naturally took sides with Mr. Butt, with the utmost alacrity, on the point in dispute.

This, of course, did not make more smooth the pathway of the two incriminated members, more especially as it gave the good-for-nothings the very excuse they wanted for staying away from any divisions Mr. Parnell or Mr. Biggar might wish to take. Yet, on the other hand, it appears to have shamed the party into fits of action now and again; as when, on the 1st of May, by offering a prolonged resistance in the Parnell manner they compelled the Government to raise the number of the committee, on cattle plague and importation of live stock, from twenty-three to twenty-seven, for the purpose of adding to it four men of the Irish party; and likewise forced them to put on the roll of the committee a couple of names which had been at first rejected. Still further, throughout the greater part of the session the members for Meath and Cavan received most valuable aid at critical moments from some half-dozen of their colleagues, including Major O'Gorman, Major Nolan, Mr. A. M. Sullivan, Mr. O'Connor Power, and Mr. G. H. Kirk.

Mr. Butt about April wrote a lengthy letter to Mr. Biggar, and subsequently another long one to Mr. Parnell, on the subject of their new patent breechloading weapon for attacking the British House of Commons. As these letters did not produce the effect for which they were ostensibly intended, he most unwisely hastened to publish them. There can be no doubt that they were originally written with a view to eventual publication. They were couched in a style meant rather for the Irish people at large than for the two gentlemen addressed. Mr. Parnell replied in an

extremely able and convincing letter, intended
just as plainly for Mr. Butt's eyes only. Before,
however, it was quite finished, Mr. Parnell was
amazed to see both the communication he had
himself received and that which had been for-
warded to Mr. Biggar appearing in the columns
of the Irish press. This circumstance of course
left Mr. Parnell no option but to publish his reply.
At that time it had been the fashion with many
people who conceived themselves very owls for
wisdom to speak of Mr. Parnell as a well meaning
young man, but very headstrong and imprudent.
We reprint here the conclusion of this letter, from
which readers may be able to judge for themselves
whether the balance of prudence in this controversy lay on the side of Mr. Butt or of Mr.
Parnell. The passage is as follows :—

"P. S.—Since writing much of the above I find
that your action in publishing your letter to Mr.
Biggar, and subsequently that to myself, will necessi-
tate the publication of this my reply. I regard your
conduct in thus appealing to the public upon a matter
which you have never even yet brought under the consideration of the Parliamentary party as most precipi-
tate and deplorable, and well calculated to lead to
serious dissension ; but as you have taken the step I
must disclaim for myself the responsibility of any
damage which the knowledge of the serious charges
contained in my letter may do to the Home Rule party
in the minds of the public.

"C. S. P."

Throughout all this controversy and others that followed between the parties, not one uncourteous word fell from Mr. Parnell's lips or pen in respect to Isaac Butt. He conducted his arguments with unimpeachable gentlemanliness throughout; and even when the great old man, then fast declining towards the grave, had sunk in the popular estimation, Mr. Parnell never wrote or spoke of him a single syllable that could rankle in his heart or cause him a personal pang. The consequence was that till the last, however much he disapproved of his policy, Isaac Butt cherished a sincere respect for Mr. Parnell.

As was to be expected, Mr. Butt's attacks on Messrs. Parnell and Biggar, and their defences, when given to the public, created no little sensation, not only in Ireland, but in Great Britain also. The press of the latter country patted the leader of the Home Rule party on the back, and found out numerous good qualities in him which it had not before discovered. There was joy in the British camp; for was not the old delightful game of Irish dissension being played as charmingly as ever? Mr. Butt was a very distinguished man; he had experience; he knew what "the tone of the House" was; he respected its traditions; his great ability enabled him to see how damaging even to Irish interests was the course on which Parnell and his friends, men without brains or experience, had entered; though un-

fortunately he had lent himself to a scheme
which threatened "the integrity of the empire,"
he was yet at heart a constitutionalist. Such
was the style of comment bestowed on him by
his new patrons, the London editors; and as, in
truth, he really believed the most of it, his anx-
iety to shackle the active men was not thereby
lessened.

In Ireland, however, a widely different kind of
comment began to prevail. Though in the pro-
British and the trimming journals abuse or depre-
cation of "obstruction" was a staple topic, all
the organs of national opinion which had earned
a character for honesty in the past encouraged
Mr. Parnell and his auxiliaries to persevere.
Elderly people, wealthy people, "loyal" people,
and people by nature timid, in addition to the
old women of both sexes, alarmed by Mr. Butt's
denunciations of the new policy as "revolutionary," shrieked out against it; but the mass of the
nation, who in all probability saw nothing in it
then but a means of punishing the British Parliament for its confirmed hostility to Irish rights,
promptly ranged themselves on the side of Parnell and Biggar. In this state of affairs Mr.
Butt, having failed to achieve the purpose intended by the publication of his letters to those
gentlemen, convened for the 16th of June a meeting of the Irish Parliamentary party to take the
"obstruction" question into consideration.

Meanwhile, undeterred by the storms gathering around them from opposite quarters, the few adherents of this "revolutionary" policy went steadily on in their course. As at a bull-baiting the remorseless dog seizes his enormous antagonist by the lip, pinning his head to the ground, and with iron jaws holds him immovable and helpless, so they held the House of Commons in an inexorable gripe, overmastering, persistent, unrelaxing. The House might bellow as much as it liked, and bellow outrageously it did pretty often, but that was nearly the utmost it could do. Now Mr. Parnell worried it on the question of the release of the political prisoners; now on the corrupting employment of secret service money in Ireland; now on the Irish Judicature Bill; now on the Irish County Courts Bill; now on the army estimates; and so on. Whatever the measure the Government might bring on, a watchful wide-awake Irish half-dozen were present to see that it received proper discussion. And here it may be remarked that one of the rare occasions on which Mr. Parnell was called to order occurred in a contest with the House on the 1st of May, 1877, over the nomination of Mr. Biggar to a place on the cattle-plague inquiry committee. Some paltry snob of an Englishman had the audacity to sneer at Mr. Biggar for being in trade. At this insult to his fast friend and consistent colleague the hidden fire of Mr. Parnell's nature

flamed forth. That mode of personal attack is
essentially an offensively vulgar one ; while Charles
Stewart Parnell, from the crown of his head to
the sole of his foot, is a gentleman every inch.
In denouncing the British snob the warmth of his
feelings caused him to forget his customary prudence, and he twice fell foul of the "rules of the
House." Very few gentlemen of any country
would think anything the worse of him for this
rare exhibition of loss of perfect self-control.
Most Irishmen, we fancy, would emphatically
pronounce the throwing of prudence to the winds
under such circumstances to be " a good fault."

Once again, a little later on, he was hurried into
excitement during a debate on the Irish political
prisoners. Home Secretary Cross had denied
that there were any then in durance. The Fenian
soldiers still held he described as military prisoners; O'Meara Condon and Melody as murders;
and Mr. Michael Davitt as an ordinary convict.
Such a classification of men, whose real crime in
British eyes was notoriously their connection with
an organization which aimed at the overthrow of
British rule in Ireland, stung Mr. Parnell to the
quick; therefore he rose to reply to Mr. Cross,
and to expose his misrepresentations. Although a
newspaper correspondent described him on that
occasion as speaking " with the placidity and gen-
tleness of demeanor, and in the cultivated accents,
which are the marvel of strangers who are shown

for the first time the terrible twin obstructive," the outward calm but hid a volcanic working beneath, and after a few sharp sentences, brimming over with indignation, yet couched in language of the kind considered not inadmissible in that temple of manners, the London House of Commons, he was compelled by the strength of his emotions to bring his remarks to a close with the statement that he could not trust himself to speak further. And the stolid British majority, who had been accustomed to think him in nature as not unlike one of themselves, incapable of warm sympathies or generous feelings, received that statement with derisive shouts of "Oh!" The broader purpose of working out his tactics skilfully — the only way in which they could be worked — made him check himself before he had infringed his privileges as a member of Parliament; and in a little while after, on the same night, he was able to assail, with the most absolute self-control, but with a sharpness which was certainly not blunted by Secretary Cross' earlier observations on Irish political prisoners, the whole system of spies and "informers" in Ireland, in a debate which he raised on the estimates for "secret service money."

The 16th of June came; and oh! what a flocking to the London chambers of the Irish party there was of its members. It had got bruited among them that Parnell and Biggar and the other troublesome persons who wanted activity

and earnestness and courage in Irish members of
Parliament were now at last to be definitely
squelched. Men whom the most urgent requisi-
tion of their leader could not bring thither when
it was only a question of taking counsel how best
to forward some Irish interest in Parliament, were
prompt in attendance when the object in view was
the highly important one of annihilating such ex-
hibitions of zeal in the country's service as were a
standing reproach to those members who did not
care one jot about the country or its interests so
long as confiding constituencies could be found to
elect political hypocrites to represent them.   The
do-nothings turned up in alarming force at the
meeting, now at last resolved to "do something"
—not for Ireland; oh! no! but for the ridding
their own precious selves of a perpetual annoy-
ance.   The contrast between activity and indo-
lence, between earnestness and indifference, between steady application to Parliamentary duty
and almost equally steady neglect of it — this was
setting up a totally new example, establishing an
alarming precedent, instilling into the minds of
Irish electors the pernicious notion that they
ought to expect real service from their representatives; and of course the sooner such a mon-
strous conception of political duty was smothered
the better.   To those London chambers of the
Irish party also crowded the old Whigs who had
masqueraded as Home Rulers at the general

election of 1874, and who, so long as a Tory Government was in office, might be depended on to appear pretty constantly in opposition to it — whether as followers of Isaac Butt or of the Marquis of Hartington mattered but little for the time. To the same chamber came also the more limited number of Tories who had donned the Home Rule cloak to secure election, but who were equally anxious with the two other classes to put down the men that were lunatic or idiotic enough to keep Ireland — Ireland only — in view in the British Parliament.

Yet it is somewhat consoling to remember that a very considerable number of the Irish Parliamentary party who were not able conscientiously to accept the new policy, or did not quite understand all its bearings, made it their business to attend this meeting of the 16th of June, 1877, to interpose themselves between the "too active" minority and the too idle majority. Their well-meant services, however, were not needed at the time. Isaac Butt was no fool. He found on this occasion forty of his nominal followers surrounding him — a number by far greater than he could ordinarily gather around him in what he deemed crises of the very first importance in Irish affairs. He knew, too, how reedlike was the support afforded him by many of those who had answered with such unusual alacrity his present summons. And he knew that the one complaint he had to make

against the Parnell and Biggar handful was what
he unfortunately considered too much zeal.   Consequently, when they explained the motives which
had moved them in the Parliamentary action to
which he took exception, and corrected the false
impression of it which he had conceived, there
was an end for the moment of all controversy.
No resolution condemnatory of them was passed ;
but instead was one inculcating the need of more
frequent meetings of the party, so as to secure
more unity and greater activity in its proceedings.
Vain hopes ! delusive dreams !   Wild horses, un-
tamed elephants, could not have dragged back
again to those chambers wherein that resolution
was unanimously voted several of those who assented to it that day.   They had gone there to
assist in putting down inconvenient activity ; in
the turn that affairs took they were left only the
alternative of exposing their hypocrisy or agree-
ing to the resolution ; they chose the latter course,
but apparently with a mental reservation which
gave them liberty to exempt themselves from the
scope of the resolution.   At all events, the rooms
of the party were but seldom afterwards enlightened with their presence.

The wonderful effect of this famous meeting in
restraining those whom it was called together to
handcuff will presently be seen.   A few days after
it was held, however, an event happened which
contributed to give some extraordinary develop-

ments to the new Irish policy in the British Parliament.   This was the election of Mr. Frank
Hugh O'Donnell as member for Dungarvan on
the 23d of June, 1877.

Mr. O'Donnell was a graduate of the Queen's
College, Galway, and a man of varied accomplishments and much ability, who had gravitated
towards the London press. For years he had
waged relentless war against the mixed system of
education, especially as illustrated in the Queen's
Colleges; and year after year he had undevi-
atingly attended the convocation of the Queen's
University to assail, generally single-handed, in
the teeth of an adverse majority, its fundamental
principle.   As he never had more than one sup-
porter on these occasions, and usually had not
even one; and as the other members of convocation, from the occupant of the chair to the youngest graduate, were zealous adherents of the
"mixed system," it is easy to see what hardihood
he must have had to stand up for the right in a
gathering so completely adverse, and to fancy
what hootings, jeerings, clamor of all kinds — to
say nothing of perpetual calls to order by the
chairman — he had to endure.

One who had received such rough but suitable
training was eminently a man for the new Parliamentary policy; and as if by natural instinct Mr.
O'Donnell took to it.   He became at once, and
continued to be, one of the most efficient of Mr.

Parnell's aids. There was no fear whatever that the wildest tumult of the London Commons would put him down. As the stormy petrel is at home when elemental fury is at its highest, so was Mr. O'Donnell amid the hurricane rage of a bitterly hostile assembly.

He had formally taken his seat but a few days when he gave his fellow Commoners a taste of his quality. The date was the night of the 2nd July, or rather the morning of the 3d. The hour was one o'clock. The occasion was the wish of the few watchful, industrious Irish members present to protest against the denial to Ireland of volunteer corps. The opportunity afforded was the vote for the British volunteers in the army estimates.

At one o'clock in the morning, Captain Nolan (who has since attained the rank of Major), whose courage and fidelity are worthy of all honor, opened the ball by moving "that the chairman do report progress." His object was to secure the bringing on of the vote for the British volunteers at an hour when a discussion on the Irish side of the question could be raised with effect; it being notorious that in the small hours of the morning the British Commons are utterly impatient of and adverse to discussion, wanting to have done with business of any kind, however important, and to go home to bed; and it being almost equally notorious that Government business which is likely to evoke discussion, comes on, by some singular chance, at those same small hours.

And here it may be remarked that the essence of what is now commonly called the Parnell policy consists in having, on every occasion when it is brought in play, a distinct, appreciable, and reasonable purpose. Its strength lies in the fact that, while every form of Parliament is to be availed of, nothing is to be done blindly, or without an object readily comprehensible by at least the leaders of the House. It is elastic also as well as strong, for it can be employed on every variety of topic that can come before the Commons at Westminster. Also—since the Union compels the return of Irish members to the British Parliament—so long as the Union lasts (and that is to say, so long as Irish members are sent to that Parliament), there is no possible way of checking the employment of that policy, even a little, except by restricting the liberties of British members themselves. For the Act of Union puts Irish members on precisely the same footing as those of Great Britain; and any distinction made between them would tear up the last shred of that Act. Even the alternative of ejecting from the House obnoxious individual Irish members, while a precedent full of evil possibilities for the British themselves, would be useless in presence of a determined spirit in the Irish constituencies; since the seats made vacant could be easily filled — and

would certainly be in such circumstances — by
men who would very soon be at least as obnoxious.
Again, with half a hundred members working in
concert on the principles invented by Mr. Parnell,
it would even be impossible to single out individual members for censure or punishment; and
therefore a really resolute Irish party might triumphantly exclaim to the most intolerant British
majority that ever existed since 1801, "Now, infi-
del, I have thee on the hip!" In short, even to
cripple "obstruction," carried out systematically
and skilfully by only a score of members acting
on a common understanding, the majority must
cripple themselves also, must part with valuable
priviliges, materially impair not only the prestige
and the freedom of the London Parliament, but
its strength as a bulwark of English liberties as
well, and surrender portion of its power of resisting the encroachments of tyranny.

There were over a hundred British members in
the House, the Home Rulers were but seven in all,
when Captain Nolan rose to his feet. The British majority resented the intrusion of Irish members in their affairs. But the Irish, few as they
were, were resolved to win. Captain Nolan
having withdrawn his motion, Mr. O'Connor
Power took it up. Of course he was beaten on a
division. Mr. O'Donnell promptly rose to move
"that the chairman do leave the chair." A hideous din greeted him as he went on to speak to

his motion. Some of the gentlemen of "the first assembly in the world" began those imitations of the speech of the lower animals at which they are such adepts; others laughed loudly in derision; others, again, indulged in inarticulate shouts; and others still, as the tremendous uproar went on, exclaimed, "let us see how much he will stand." Such terms as "hypocritical," "shabby," and such choice flowers of rhetoric as "pigs could obstruct," were bandied about amid the tumult of the night; and the chairman of committees, alarmed at the state of violent disorder to which the House in its anger had reduced itself, interposed sharply several times to restrain the more violent, and even threatened to bring the beastly conduct of one "noble lord" before the House. The great British Parliament, in fact — the model of representative institutions all over the world — had been turned for the nonce into a Bedlam.

Those who were anxious to know how much Mr. O'Donnell "could stand" soon discovered that he could stand a great deal indeed. When he had been on his legs about half an hour, and a partial lull in the storm had been obtained through the chairman's exertions, he paralyzed his British audience by coolly observing that as they had not been able to hear his remarks it would be necessary to make them over again. And he was as good as his word. He began his speech anew, and unconcernedly went over the whole ground he

had before traversed; and when at a quarter past
two he resumed his seat he had infused into the
breasts of his would-be tormentors a feeling lu-
dicrously akin to positive terror.

The House had been gradually receiving acces-
sions during these proceedings until the majority
reached about one hundred and fifty. The Irish
still fought on. Some British members, unwilling
to give way to the audacious Hibernian handful, yet
anxious to go home, had the House "counted,"
but when forty members were found to be present
the sitting went on. Major O'Gorman followed
Mr. O'Donnell with a motion "that the chairman
report progress;" when *he* was beaten Mr. O'Connor Power moved "that the chairman leave the
chair;" when *he* was beaten Mr. Richard Power
moved that progress be reported; when *he* was
beaten Mr. Parnell moved the chairman out of the
chair; when *he* was beaten Mr. O'Connor Power
moved to report progress. Thus the British
majority were kept marching and countermarching in and out of the division lobby pretty actively
for an hour.

About this time, three o'clock having been
reached, the chairman felt that unsupported nature
could not sustain itself in such distressing circumstances, so he had refreshments brought to him
into the House, and consumed them with what
relish he could at the table in front of the chair.
The Speaker, whose office compelled him to wait

for the formal adjournment of the sitting, was asleep in another chamber. Much talk went on, much bandying of more or less polite abuse, much crimination and recrimination ; and in the meantime the short Summer night had slipped away, the morning sun was streaming in through the windows, and at four o'clock the gas was turned off. During the talk two other efforts to count out the House had been made without effect. The marching and countermarching began again. Mr. Parnell moved to report progress ; Mr. O'Donnell that the chairman leave the chair. These were followed in quick succession by corresponding motions from Mr. O'Connor Power, Major O'Gorman, and Mr. Richard Power; when another effort to count out the House was made ; but still there were found over forty brave Britons who would perish on the spot rather than surrender.

The divisions had been going on in a grim, business-like way for an hour, when Mr. Parnell remarked that Irish questions were treated there in a half-contemptuous way, and that by determined action they would force on the House the duty of treating them properly. Whereupon an English member, rejoicing in the name of Blake, rather irrelevantly retorted that Mr. Parnell had spoken disrespectfully of Mr. Speaker ; to which charge Mr. Parnell, in calm accents, gave a "distinct denial" and "the flattest contradiction." A hurricane of uproar and confusion supervened ;

and when the chairman had calmed it down somewhat the walking in and out of the lobbies recom-
menced. Mr. Richard Power and Mr. Parnell
moved the usual motions. Another futile effort
was made for a count-out; then the division on
Mr. Parnell's motion was taken, and announced
at five minutes to seven. Mr. O'Connor Power
at once moved that progress be reported. Some
talk ensued, in the course of which Sir John
Lubbock complained that only five Irish members
pursued this unprecedented course; whereupon
Mr. Parnell enlivened matters by playfully re-
minding him that there is luck in odd numbers;
and Mr. Whalley — kindly old soul that he was,
even if sometimes wrong-headed — who had manfully stood by the Irishmen all the livelong night,
threw in a scrap of the comic element by censur-
ing Ministers for having kept them there all night
"at the risk of their lives."

The House was again counted. Only thirty-six
were found present; so the Speaker was roused
from his slumbers and came into the Commons
chamber. Having again counted the House, and
found only thirty present, he declared the sitting
adjourned.

It is now twelve minutes past seven. The
warm glare of the July morning fills the large
apartment; and there, "like eagles in the sun,
the Irish stand," cheering loudly — "the field is
fought and won." They have gained their point.

By sheer resolution and endurance they have beaten the domineering British majority.

As may be supposed, the all-night contest of the 3rd July, and the Irish victory in which it resulted, roused to a white heat of fury the indignant blood of every true Briton. "If this kind of thing is to go on," was the universal cry from Land's End to John-o'-Groats, "what is to become of the most venerated of our institutions? Parliament will be brought into permanent contempt; its prestige is already fearfully lowered; its *morale* has even now received alarming shocks from which it must take time to recover; and where will it all end if 'obstruction' be persisted in? Why, the Irish will be virtual dictators of the House. They will destroy it altogether, or compel it to let go its grasp on their country."

British editors, in especial, saw all this quite clearly, and for weeks did not tire of ringing the changes on it. Not only in the London but in the provincial press rabid leaders against "the obstructives" were every-day occurrences. "Obstruction" should be put down with a high hand; it should be stamped out, etc., etc. This was the burden of their monotonous song. But how? The question was a greater puzzle than the riddle of the Sphinx in the antique days. All the writers sagely and solemnly asseverated that "*something* should be done;" but not one of them could discover what that something could possibly be. The incriminated members had simply exercised the privileges of their position. It was patent that to punish them for so doing would not only wear an ugly look in foreign eyes, but would establish a bad precedent which might afterwards be employed to the detriment of British liberties. There could be no possibility of hiding from the nations abroad aught in connection with scenes which had attracted the gaze of the civilized world; nor does history offer any guarantee that there may not soon arise a designing British Minister of Imperial proclivities, misleading genius, and mastery of base arts, who, backed by a blind majority, would not scruple to use any weapon he found ready to his grasp to crush a handful struggling in the House of Commons to preserve the rights so hardly won for themselves by the British people. Therefore the efforts made to crack the exceedingly hard nut of "obstruction" got no farther in the press than that "something should be done."

But if the editors were furious, what term can describe the feelings surging in the breasts of the mass of members of Parliament? If howling and clamor, and all the ways of a cowardly mob, short of actual personal violence, could vanquish the Irish enemy, there would have been a speedy end to the trouble. Those rude weapons, however, had been tried and been found of no avail. Nevertheless it was clear that "something should be done;" so the active brain of one Mr. Puleston —

who strangely blends in himself British membership, Yankee birth and connections, and violent
Tory leanings — was set to work.

On the 4th of July he came down to the House
with what he thought was an eighty-ton gun,
warranted to blow up " the obstructives " at a
single discharge, and all his own invention too.
Its charmingly simple principle was to entrust to
a majority of the House of Commons the power of
crushing a minority at will.   But this monster
piece of ordnance, while no doubt very effective
for the purpose Mr. Puleston had in mind, was
unfortunately too sweeping in its discharge; and
could not be counted on to avoid blowing up
others than mere Irish members.   The House very
soon saw that this was the case ; and the consequence was that Mr. Puleston's eighty-ton gun
was rejected amid general laughter.

The English Tory of the name of Blake — perhaps smarting under that " flattest contradiction "
which he had received from Mr. Parnell on the
morning of the 3rd — returned to the charge on
the 4th, burning for the opportunity of bringing
the member for Meath to book about his alleged
disrespectful language concerning the Speaker of
the House.   Being on that occasion foiled he
made another essay on the 5th.   The forms of the
House stood in his way ; but Mr. Parnell was
quite anxious to accommodate Mr. Blake ; and,
rising in his place, blandly observed that if the

House wished for explanation on the matter, "he did not in any way wish to stand in the way of the House getting that explanation." The Speaker himself closed the incident for the time; but on the 6th Mr. Parnell made an early opportunity for giving his explanation, and so disposed of Mr. Blake and his motion.

The same night, Mr. Biggar and he, as composed as if nothing had ever happened out of the usual course, and as if they had not been besides the theme of numberless hostile leading articles in the papers for several mornings, quite calmly and deliberately opposed two English bills, taking several divisions on motions to stop their progress in committee, and in the end were again victorious. Further, some English "gentleman" having spoken of Mr. Biggar as a "blackguard" during the struggle, Mr. Parnell had him at once before the Speaker, and compelled him to withdraw and apologize for using the offensive epithet.

About this period the Government was very anxious to push on two Irish measures of its own — the Judicature Bill and the County Courts Bill — many of the provisions of both of which had earned the condemnation of the Irish Parliamentary party, or, to speak more correctly, of such of them as took the trouble to attend even moderately to their public duties. Whenever any of the party were inclined for work, Mr. Parnell worked with them heartily. In conjunction with

them he took an active part in the issues raised on
the Judicature Bill, besides dragging up the
Phœnix Park outrage on the estimates for the
metropolitan police; making efforts to improve
the constitution of the Local Government Board;
and again drawing attention to the Phœnix Park
outrage on the constabulary estimates. He succeeded in procuring the adoption of several of his
amendments, as well as in extracting from the
Government a definite promise that they would
provide for independent inspection of all convict
prisons, so that their unhappy inmates should not
be left wholly to the tender mercies of hardened
officials. Good work for a single man, this will
no doubt be thought; yet not a tithe of what it
would have been but for the restraining presence
of Mr. Butt, who appealed to Mr. Parnell to give
way on the constabulary estimates. In spite of
what had passed between the two gentlemen, Mr.
Parnell, in deference to Mr. Butt, did give way.
Thus a "scene" which must have been more violent than any preceding one, was avoided on the
19th of July; for it had been Mr. Parnell's resolve to have challenged a division on every one
of thirty-two estimates, and it is but natural to
suppose that the tempers of the mob of unwilling pedestrians should have suffered more than
ever under an infliction so unprecedented. Mr.
Parnell, however, did not leave the House in the
least doubt either as to the intentions he had en-

tertained or the reason which moved him to forego them. He openly stated that "it was fortunate for the Government that the honorable and learned member for Limerick was present; for, had it not been for his declared wish, he (Mr. Parnell) should have divided the House on every one of the thirty-two votes." A sense of relief must have been experienced all along the Government benches at this announcement, and a transitory feeling of gratitude to Mr. Butt no doubt was felt. Against Mr. Parnell, on the other hand, the bitterest antipathy was excited by his audacious declaration. It was borne in mind too; and the very next night the frantic hostility of "the first assembly of gentlemen in the world," as the English are fond of calling their House of Commons, burst in a tornado of uproar, the equal of which had never been known within the walls of the Commons chamber. The scene which took place was similar to those we have previously described, only much more disorderly, tumultuous, and disgraceful.

The scene began by Mr. Biggar moving, near one o'clock in the morning, that progress should be reported. In the course of an animated discussion which ensued, Mr. Butt said he did not regard the proceedings initiated by Mr. Biggar as obstruction. Notwithstanding this pronouncement of the leader of the Irish party, Mr. Meldon "protested against the course taken by the

honorable member for Cavan as obstructive," etc.
Mr. O'Shaughnessy also, the junior member for
Limerick city, was rewarded by "loud cheers,"
for a wanton attack upon his brother Irish members. This brought Mr. Parnell to his feet in reply. Then the full fury of the hurricane burst
forth. The uproar grew deafening. Most of it
was inarticulate noises — shouts, hoots, yells,
groans, howls — purposely made to try once
more to cow him, and at least to prevent him
from being heard. Amid the horrid din occasionally could be heard shrieks of "'vide, 'vide,"
screams of "sit down," and the like; while one
honorable gentleman, filled with an enlightened
zeal for "the tone of the House," roared out,
familiarly, "Finish up, Parnell." The member
for Meath, however, was not cowed, did not sit
down, and would not "finish up." Instead, he
showed a spice of resentment at the organized
clamor to which he was being subjected, and contrived to make himself distinctly heard while
uttering some stinging sentences not complimentary to the English national character. But it
was hard work to go on. The following para-
graph will help the reader to realize the circumstances under which Mr. Parnell spoke that
night : —

"This is a sample (great uproar) — this is a
sample — (deafening uproar) — this is a sample of
your English fair play — (indescribable confusion).

I have often heard of it—(continued uproar)—but I have never seen it"—(prolonged uproar). In the midst of the hideous and disgusting confusion the chairman's voice is faintly heard, calling on the honorable member for Meath to proceed; to which that honorable member calmly responds that he will if he is allowed.

In the end, by persistence, Mr. Parnell won. The very means designed to prevent what was called "obstruction of business" proved in truth an admirable instrument for preventing the House from doing any business whatever. This fact began to dawn on the Tory leaders when a couple of hours had been spent in wild confusion; and at length the Chancellor of the Exchequer consented to close the sitting. It was considerably after two o'clock on a Saturday morning when the House adjourned, on the understanding that there should be a sitting for that day, beginning at noon, to push on the Judicature Bill. Saturday, except on very extraordinary occasions, is a holiday with the London Parliament, and members are always very loath to give it up to business, however important; but in the temper of the time most of the Commons were prepared to make large sacrifices in the hope of squelching the little band of irrepressible Irishmen who presumed to air opinions of their own in that assembly, and who, not content with spurning incorporation, either with the Tory party or the Whig,

actually dared to refuse assent to the notions entertained, however thoughtlessly or blindly, by an
overwhelming British majority.

For a whole week subsequently every sitting
had its "scene." The formal sitting of Saturday,
the 21st, came, and with it a mob of British members prepared to send through committee at racing
speed the Government Judicature Bill. Their
good intentions, however, were all in vain. At
the very outset they were met by a motion to report progress; and then through long weary hours
the wrangle between majority and minority went
on. It must be said of this day's sitting that by
no means such violence was displayed as at any
of the stormy night scenes; a circumstance largely
due, no doubt, to the fact that it was held before
dinner, not after.

Mr. Butt made a remarkable intervention in
the tedious debate. He began by saying that "he
rose with feelings of humiliation to take part in
this miserable discussion." Although the gist of
his speech was a condemnation of his own too
zealous followers, he did not wholly acquit the
majority of blame. The portion of his remarks
first alluded to evoked "loud cheers" of course
from the British; but they did not appreciate the
second portion at all — which was only what
might have been expected. In spite of his influential interference the Saturday sitting might
almost as well not have been held. But little

was done except to expose more clearly than ever the utter helplessness of the British House of Commons in the grasp of a few resolute Irish members.

The sitting of Monday, the 23rd, came, and the Chancellor of the Exchequer rose early in his place to propose, in view of the alarmingly backward state of "the business of the House," that Tuesdays and Wednesdays — the days devoted to the bills of private members — should be given up by them to the Government for the rest of the session. Mr. Parnell, "who rose amid loud and general interruption," opposed the Chancellor's proposition, and in the course of his speech took occasion to point out that the House was really overburdened with work; that in its insatiable appetite for meddling with the affairs of other peoples it had gorged itself with business; and that the only remedy for its complaint was disgorgement. He was informed that he must not discuss the question of Home Rule for Ireland on a motion for facilitating the transaction of "the business of the House," but he adroitly drove home his point by saying that it would be necessary very soon to take into consideration the breaking up of the legislative functions of the House, and their redistribution among smaller bodies. That day there was another scene, of course. The majority were in such a condition of mind that they could not keep their tempers for

fifteen minutes at a time; but as the climax of
violence had been reached in the sitting of the
20th, the tendency now was towards outbursts of
wrath less unreasoning. Mr. Parnell's share in
the inevitable "scene" was a warm interposition
in defence of Mr. O'Donnell when that gentleman
was grossly attacked by a Tory named Chaplin.

An incident of a very peculiar kind occurred in
the sitting of Tuesday, the 24th July, which,
though it caused much laughter in the House at
the moment, was yet added to the long list of
offences of which in the minds of most of the
British members Mr. Parnell had been guilty.
The Irish County Courts Bill was under consideration in committee; the hour was one well into
Wednesday morning. Major O'Gorman moved
that progress should be reported. He named
Mr. Biggar for his co-teller. The two gentlemen
proceeded to the lobby of the "ayes" to count
those who were of opinion that progress should
be reported. They were followed into the lobby
by but one solitary member — Mr. Parnell.
Messrs O'Gorman and Biggar had small trouble
in fulfilling their duties as tellers. Not so the
Tory whips; for when the numbers were announced there appeared "ayes," 1; "noes," 147.

The gallant major was still unsatisfied. No
sooner was the result of the division given to the
House than he moved "that the chairman do now
leave the chair." Again he named Mr. Biggar to

aid him in counting; again that gentleman cheer-
fully assented; and again Mr. Parnell rose quietly
from his seat, and placidly walked alone into the
lobby. When the division on this second motion
of Major O'Gorman's was declared, it was found
that there was but one "aye" against 128 "noes."
There was something so unique, so sublimely
audacious, in these two unprecedented divisions,
that for the nonce the British saw only a comic
side to the affair, and the announcements of the
numbers were received with roars of laughter.
But, judging from what happened on the following
day, it would seem, after all, to have been bitterly remembered.

The Government had a bill in hands for forming a confederation in their South African colonies. They had also annexed, in a most unjusti-
fiable manner, the republic of the Transvaal.
Mr. O'Donnell had put down on the notice paper
some forty amendments to the South African
Confederation Bill. On Wednesday, the 25th
of July, as soon as the House was made, he
moved to report progress, on the ground that the
Government had given no clear and satisfactory
explanation of the annexation of the Transvaal.
As usual, he was greeted with shouts and interruptions, and appeals to the chair to declare him
out of order. When he had finished, Mr. Parnell rose amid interruptions, which were repeated
and continued while he spoke. His observations

were couched in a warmer style than was habitual to him, for the subject was one on which he felt strongly. In the course of his speech he said:—

"I feel as an Irishman, coming from a country which has experienced to the fullest extent the result of English interference in its affairs, and the consequences of English cruelty and tyranny, that I have a special interest in thwarting and preventing the designs of Government upon their unfortunate South African colonists."

No sooner were these words spoken than Sir Stafford Northcote sprang to his feet like a man who saw an opportunity for which he had been looking. He moved that Mr. Parnell's words should be taken down, and the Speaker of the House sent for. These grave ceremonies having been properly performed, the words were duly reported to the Speaker. That functionary "turned eagerly upon Mr. Parnell for an explanation, but Mr. Parnell placidly looked on, and made no sign of rising. After being more than once invited to speak, the honorable member at length rose, and soon all the previous excitement was child's play to what ensued. In the most determined manner he defended himself, and, using language which greatly irritated the Ministerialists, he was called upon by the Speaker to desist and withdraw."

When a member of the London Parliament is about to be tried by his peers, the strange custom

of the place is to send him out and try him behind
his back.   Mr. Parnell left the House proper, as
desired, and proceeded to one of the galleries,
where he quietly sat observing all that subsequently passed below.   We take from a London
correspondent the following description of the
scene which ensued : —

"The moment Mr. Parnell had gone, the Chancellor
improved the opportunity by giving his version of the
occurrence, and ended by making a proposal — that
Mr. Parnell, having wilfully and persistently obstructed
public business, be suspended from the service of the
House until Friday next. . In his hasty and feeble way
it was at once seen that the Chancellor had not hit the
mark at which he aimed, and a murmur of triumphant
satisfaction ran along the Irish ranks — now greatly
recruited when it was found that a deliberate onslaught
had been made on one of their number.   Mr. Sullivan,
ever ready to fill the Irish gap, sprang to the rescue of
the member for Meath, adopted for himself the very
words which had disturbed the soul of Sir Stafford
Northcote, and challenged the Government to take *his*
words down.   With exquisite perception of the truth,
Mr. Sullivan demonstrated to the House that which
was clear enough, indeed, to those who had watched
the entire tactics of the Government throughout the
day — namely, that the Chancellor wished to punish
Mr. Parnell, not for what he had said that day, but for
his conduct on previous occasions, and which was not
on record.   Another heavy blow came upon the Government from a quarter they little suspected.   Who
was it that dared from the front Opposition bench

directly facing Mr. Hardy, to cast in the teeth of that very Hotspur of obstruction his famous avowal to 'thwart' all the efforts of the late Ministry to carry out its army reforms? Mr. Knatchbull-Hugessen, ex-Lord of the Treasury, and ex-Under Secretary for the Home Department. It was in vain that the chairman peered through his spectacles, or nervously wrung his hands. It was in vain that, with the hot blood rushing up to his face, Mr. Hardy impatiently shook his head. Mr. Hugessen dilated with great precision on the well-remembered tactics, and not once or twice, but on dozens of occasions, of members of the present Government to obstruct the measures of the late Ministry. The discussion then became general, and it was soon made apparent that the mine sprung by the Government so far had been sprung in vain. The Chancellor at last was compelled slowly to give ground, for the Speaker announced that Mr. Parnell was entitled to take his place in the House until Friday."

So the consideration of the Chancellor's penal proposal against Mr. Parnell was postponed for two days, when that most aggravating of Irish members was at last to be brought to book, to the great joy of the now triumphant majority.

"The battle is not always to the strong," according to the proverb; and in the encounter between Mr. Parnell and the Chancellor of the Exchequer, supported as the latter was by the mass of the Commons, the wise paradox received ample justification. The Chancellor was worsted, and knew that he was. So, too, knew every man in the

House who still retained even a remnant of reason. The member for Meath, calmly survey-ing from the gallery overhead the remarkable scene taking place on the floor beneath him, heard the Speaker's decision that he was at liberty to resume his place in the House. Thereupon he left the gallery, and walked quietly towards the bench usually occupied by him. Though aware that he had won an undoubted victory, and that he had had besides the gratification of opening out his mind about the Ministerialists pretty freely to them, he wore no air of triumph as he went up the floor. Rather, indeed, his mien was that of gentlemanly, if not studied, unostentation.

He did not, however, take his seat when he went in. He had had possession of the floor at the time of the Chancellor's interruption; he had not been allowed to conclude his speech; and now, after the lapse of an hour spent in dis-cussing his words and conduct, he proceeded to finish the remarks he had originally intended to make. He went on, in truth, precisely as if there had been no interruption whatever; and he amazed all, while amusing many, by taking up his speech at the exact point where he had left off — absolutely at the very words where he had been checked — "and," says a newspaper correspon-dent of the time, "bore himself with all the calmness of a judge amid the uproar."

The Marquis of Hartington, leader of the Whig

Opposition, and possible leader of the House in the event of a change of Ministry, was naturally as anxious to quell Mr. Parnell as Sir Stafford Northcote himself could be; but he was just as anxious that that should be done without at the same time doing vital injury to the House of Commons itself. Therefore, as Sir Stafford had placed himself in a false position by his rashness of the 25th July, the Marquis obligingly came to his aid at the sitting of Thursday, the 26th, by mildly suggesting that the personal aspect of the obstruction question should be wholly dropped. A capital suggestion this was for the Chancellor, seeing that he could have made nothing of his charge against Mr. Parnell; so Sir Stafford in the most amiable manner adopted the idea of his right honorable friend the noble marquis, and announced that instead of proceeding against the honorable member for Meath on the morrow he would bring forward some resolutions dealing in a general way with the facilitation of "the business of the House." In all probability this little Parliamentary farce, which went off with great *eclat*, had been arranged beforehand between the right honorable baronet and the equally right honorable marquis.

The morrow came, Friday, the 27th July, and the resolutions of the Chancellor were duly put before the House. One provided that if a member were twice declared out of order by the

Speaker or the chairman of committees, it should
be in the power of the House to muzzle him by
suspending the debate and summarily silencing
him during the remainder of the sitting. The
other provided that it should not be in the power
of any member to move more than once that the
chairman do report progress, or that the chairman
do leave the chair. The first as well as the second
of these rules was meant to work practically only
while the House sat in committee, for then it was
that the new Irish scheme of Parliamentary tactics
could be best developed.

Hours on hours of discussion of these proposals
followed their introduction; for the more thoughtful among the British members were loath to part,
even for the remainder of the session, with valuable privileges of which they themselves might
be anxious to avail themselves at any moment.
The one circumstance of the discussion which as-
tonished and disturbed the faithful Commons was,
that all the prominent "obstructives" rose to tell
the House that they had not the faintest idea of
offering opposition to the proposed rules. It had
naturally been expected that they would resist to
the utmost what was so transparently an effort to
make a net in which to catch them; and when,
instead of resisting, they seemed rather to enjoy
the process of manufacture going on before their
eyes, an uneasy feeling began to prevail in the
bosom of many a British member that the Chan-

cellor's meshes would prove unequal to their purpose. Nevertheless the Minister's blindly obedient majority obeyed his will, and the Chancellor's proposals at length became formally "rules of the House" for the rest of the session of 1877. Here we may state, however, that the only one who came under the operation of either of them was a British member—poor Mr. Whalley, to wit—and that in applying the first rule to him the Speaker made a ludicrous blunder which put his own proceeding wholly out of order, and brought down general ridicule on "the new rules." What effect those rules had in restraining "the obstructives" will presently be seen.

The sessions of the London Parliament usually close before the middle of August, to allow of noble lords and honorable and right honorable gentlemen being on the moors in time for the opening of the shooting season — an arrangement which is obviously less for the convenience of legislation than of the legislators. Lo! August was at hand, and the Government's pet project, the South African Confederation Bill, had still to go through most of its stages. Ministers felt that "something must be done" in earnest at this conjuncture. Monday, the 30th July, passed away, and the South African Bill, had virtually made no progress. The dreadful member for Dungarvan and his small band of colleagues stood in the way. Need it be said that Mr. Parnell was one of them?

Tuesday, the 31st July, disclosed the notable "something" which had been evolved.

Anything better calculated to render Parliamentary institutions worthless, to bring them into just contempt, and to make men inclined to turn from them towards some form of intelligent despotism, can hardly be conceived than the plan put in force on the 31st July. The Conservative members were divided into batches, each batch told off to appear in the House during certain hours of the evening and night. Thus a system of relays was constituted, whose duty it was to relieve each other at stated periods, and so avoid too much fatigue for any. It was perfectly understood from the first that their business was, not to discuss the provisions of the South African Bill, but to pass them. Many Whig members lent themselves to this conspiracy, moved thereto by the good old Sassenach intolerance of Irish liberties. Some of the Home Rule party, with the spaniel's instinct, did likewise. Every necessary preparation had been made to keep up the strength of the Government men. Meat and drink were provided for them regardless of expense. Supper for those who remained about the lobbies for divisions in the night, and breakfast for those expected early in the morning, were ordered by the Government whip. Such toothsome delicacies as grilled bones, devilled kidneys, and spatchcocks figured largely on the dining-room tables. Copi-

ous supplies of champagne were there to keep up
the fighting spirit of the Saxon host. No doubt
it had that effect as the hours flew by ; but it had
the effect also of making honorable members
more uproarious than they might otherwise have
been.

The struggle began at about five o'clock on
Tuesday evening, Mr. O'Donnell, in right of his
scores of amendments, leading the assault. The
Irish, all told, numbered just seven. Mr. Butt
sided with the Government and the majority, and
bitterly assailed the colleagues who were too active
for his wishes. He publicly denied in the House
that they were members of the Irish party, and
declared that if he thought their conduct received
the sanction of their countrymen he would retire
from Irish politics as from "a vulgar brawl."
Yet he should not be judged too harshly. His
early conservative training could not but have
left some warp in his ideas.

All night long the contest went on. The chairman of committees was relieved by a deputy, who
in turn was relieved by another, who in turn was
relieved by still another, who in turn was relieved
by the chairman in person. Every amendment
proposed was ignorantly defeated, when brought
to a division, by a swarm of British members who
had not heard a word of the reasons urged in favor
of the amendments, but who rushed into the
House with the sole and deliberate purpose of

voting down any and every proposal that came from the Irish seven.

As might be expected, Mr. Parnell took a conspicuous part in the fray. In the course of the night, in language which the newspaper correspondents characterized as of extraordinary boldness, he taunted the Englishmen with their love of boasting, sneered at "English fair play," told them it was best exemplified in their national custom of kicking a man when down, and described them as " big bullies," who, like all bullies, shrank when they were met with determination. It need hardly be added that such plain and truthful speaking was not at all to the taste of those who heard it ; but they had to swallow it as best they could.

This was just the occasion on which to test the value of the "new rules." Strange to say, however, the Irish members kept wonderfully within the bounds of order, while such of their British opponents as ventured to speak at all were constantly tripping up, and one after another, amid general mortification, had to withdraw and to apologize for his unparliamentary expressions. As if to crown the absurdity of the anti-obstruction devices, and to put a climax of ridicule on those doings of "the assembled wisdom of the country," the very chairman himself got out of order, made a ruling antagonistic to the Irish which was at once challenged, and was con-

strained to withdraw it and to say, "I beg your
pardon," to the infinite grief of the wildly excited
but thoroughly humiliated mob of Britishers.   To
Mr. Edmund Dwyer Gray, then in his best days
as an Irish politician, was due a result so provo-
cative of inextinguishable laughter.

The wear and tear of this most harassing session had for some time been telling on Mr. Parnell.   The London correspondent of the *Newcastle
Chronicle*, who is understood to be no other than
Mr. Joseph Cowen, M. P., for Newcastle-on-Tyne,
writing a little while before this famous scene at
Westminster, describes him as looking much worn,
and as having aged wonderfully in appearance
within a comparatively short time.   Though his
strength was failing he held on resolutely all
through the night, saw the sun rise and the gas
turned off; and not till a quarter past eight in the
morning, after fifteen hours of incessant labor,
mental and vocal, protracted struggle, unending
uproar, and unbroken excitement, did he retire
from the arena to take a much needed rest.
Others had preceded him, and had returned to
their posts.   But he did not remain long away.
Four hours later, at a quarter past twelve, he was
again by the side of his few colleagues; and
thenceforward until the last division was taken,
after a sitting of the unprecedented duration of
twenty-six hours, he continued with them the
unequal fight.

It should be noted here, as a very interesting incident of this famous sitting of the British Parliament, that Miss Fanny Parnell, one of the high-spirited sisters of the member for Meath, sat all night long in the ladies' gallery of the Commons chamber, a listener to and a spectator of what was going forward below. The lady's strong Irish sympathies and high-souled courage are very generally known by this time.

Another notable incident of the twenty-six hours' sitting may be recalled. There is a chaplain attached to the House of Commons, whose duty it is to prepare with prayer the business of each sitting — an ironical proceeding some may think. He came down to the House at twelve o'clock on Wednesday, book in hand, to perform his functions in the ordinary course at a day sitting. His astonishment may be imagined when he found the night sitting of Tuesday still in full swing at noonday on Wednesday; and he precipitately beat a retreat.

The Government had carried their point. They had forced the South African Confederation Bill through committee; but they had done so at the cost of depriving the House of Commons of all character as a deliberative assembly. Very soon they were made to know that. Every journal in Great Britain and Ireland was ringing with the twenty-six hours' fight; and though, of course, the British writers at first and chiefly showered blame on the heads of the Irish "obstructives," yet the conspirators against freedom of debate came in for the gravest censure. Englishmen are as jealous of their hard-won national liberties as they are impatient of the liberties of other peoples; and from all sides came down a very hail of denunciation on the Government for daring to overturn, by the system of "relays," the whole constitution of the House of Commons, and causing it to violate its duty of deliberating on legislative projects. Thus the latest weapon fashioned for the crushing of the new Irish tactics was discovered to be more fatal to British freedom than to "obstruction;" consequently it was never more employed.

Again, the Irish, with their accustomed skill, had selected for their operations a subject which was certain to afford them ample justification for the most strenuous opposition. The annexation of the Transvaal and the South African Confederation Act were between them responsible for the Zulu war, with its bloody episodes and its disgraceful disasters of Isandula and the Intombi river, as well as for the heavy pecuniary costs involved — costs which must come out of the pockets chiefly of British taxpayers. Nor is it by any means certain, at the time of this writing, that all trouble for the British empire is at an end in South Africa. It may be a long while ere the Boers are content to remain in that South African

Confederation with which they were so violently
incorporated.

About the beginning of August London editors made a singular discovery. They had
previously been accustomed to refer to Mr. Parnell as a man wholly without capacity, who had
achieved a bad notoriety by a series of wanton
outrages against "the tone of the House." All
of a sudden, however, they found out that he was
a man of "undoubted ability," who showed great
skill in selecting the subjects he brought before
the House aforesaid, great clearness in presenting his views, and great adroitness in utilizing
the forms of Parliament. He was spoken of
kindly as a young man who had a splendid career
open to him if he would employ his undoubted
ability in less aggravating ways, and would not
set himself in violent opposition to the House.
Why, it was hinted, he might before long actually
be a Cabinet Minister of the British Empire. A
man with his gifts might aspire to almost any
post. In other words, if he would only throw
over Ireland, accept the Union, and settle down to
work as a British party-man, he would in the end
be duly rewarded with "a place." Charles Stewart
Parnell, nevertheless, heeded as little this British
soft sawder as he heeded the uproar to which
British members of Parliament nightly treated
him. He went on his own way without pause
or falter, offering, with Mr. O'Donnell and others,

amendments to the Prisons Bill and the South African Bill to the last, some of which were so obviously valuable that the Government accepted them. Nay, a few nights after the twenty-six hours' fight he calmly "talked out" the Expiring Laws Continuance Bill — a Government measure of the very first importance — the feat evoking only unutterable horror. It was too much. Words — nay, even brayings — could not express what was felt on the occasion.

The strong language in which Mr. Butt indulged in the debate on the morning of the 1st of August expressed his real feelings, and he soon made an effort to procure the expulsion from the Irish Parliamentary party of those members who had the temerity to defy English public opinion and to show the most utter disregard for " the tone of the House." It should be remembered for him that he was then fast failing both in mind and body, that he was constitutionally averse from anything in the nature of resolute fighting, and that, besides, the training of a life, most of which was passed in *nisi prius* courts, inclined him to persuasion and argument for the accomplishment of his ends. If he were so wanting in sagacity as to regard the British Parliament as though it were an enormous jury sworn to do justice according to the evidence, there was much excuse for him. His effort to expel Mr. Parnell and his friends wholly failed at the meeting of the Irish party called for that express purpose. Even though Mr. Butt threatened to resign his leadership, if his wishes were not complied with, the meeting broke up without doing anything or coming to any decision on the question before them.

In Ireland the course pursued by Mr. Parnell and his friends was not only understood but thoroughly approved of; and when it came to be known that efforts were being made by Mr. Butt to crush the fighting men of his own following, it was deemed judicious to give him some unmistakable inkling of the popular judgment on the subject in dispute. Accordingly a public meeting in honor of Messrs. Parnell and Biggar was projected in Dublin, to be held in the historic Round Room of the Rotundo. The committee of management early foresaw that some mode of checking the rush that would be made on the room the night of the meeting was an absolute necessity. Admission by ticket only was resorted to. The demand for tickets was amazing. All classes, rich and poor, high and low, made application; even numerous civil servants eagerly sought for them that they might secure admission.

The most remarkable session of the British Parliament for over a century came to an end on the 13th of August, 1877. The Rotundo meeting followed on the 21st of the same month. Even under the ticket system every part of the vast hall — platform, floor, and gallery — was over-

crowded. The scene when the two guests of the
evening came on the platform was such as was
never previously witnessed, there or elsewhere,
by the present generation. Such wild enthusiasm, such unbounded delight, such universal
cheering, prolonged for ten minutes, such waving
of hats in air by strong-armed men, such fluttering
of snowy handkerchiefs by bright-eyed women—
such a scene as this is seldom witnessed more than
once in a life-time. A forest of hats moved to
and fro over the densely packed mass on the
great platform ; and in front of that black moving
mass there stood, erect, unwavering, a tall slight
figure, presenting a pale quiet face with set
features, which might have caused an observer to
think that their owner was stirred by no emotion
whatever, either through the thrilling sight before
him or the yet more thrilling sounds of joy and
welcome which tore the air incessantly, but that
now and again a soft light came and went in the
bright brown eyes. And when the cheering
within the room had died away, lo ! more mighty
still in volume came the hurrahing of the many
thousands outside the building, who, unable to
effect an entrance, were yet eager to join their
voices with those of the more fortunate within, in
an overpowering demonstration of welcome to
Parnell and Biggar, the two exemplars of faithful
Irish representatives. Dublin had spoken on the

issue raised by Mr. Butt, and her verdict was emphatically with Mr. Parnell.

The capital of a nation may not be in strict accord, either politically or morally, with the rest of the country. Provincial places usually move more slowly than metropolitan ones; provincial people do not catch up new ideas in a hurry. Dublin indeed had spoken; but the voice of the provinces had yet to be heard in judgment on the new Parliamentary policy before any one could assume that it had the approval of the country. Yet so rapidly did this policy commend itself to the national intelligence that within a few weeks Mr. Parnell was invited to and honored at public meetings and banquets by several provincial districts, the old fortress-town of Kilmallock spiritedly leading the way. Wherever, in fact, the people were given the opportunity of making a pronouncement, it was emphatically on the side of Parnell as against Butt.

That circumstance, however, did not prevent Mr. Butt from retaining much influential support for the "fair-and-easy" method he himself favored. He had too often branded as "revolutionary" the more active and persistent one not to have had a following among the large number of people who, in Ireland as elsewhere, shrink from a course which they regard as violent.

Nevertheless Mr. Butt must have felt that the sceptre was slipping from his grasp; that his title

of leader was scarcely more than nominal; that
his power over the Irish people, whether to spur
forward or restrain, was fast ebbing away. It
was a mortifying position for the great old man,
and its bitterness must have been aggravated by
the consciousness of failing health. His step was
even then growing slow and heavy; his great
frame, massive as an oak-tree's trunk, had fallen
far forward at the shoulders; the movement of
his big heart was feeble, and his pulses made less
healthful music than of yore. Worse than all,
the splendid intellect, once so strong and so
versatile, and on which a great question seemed
to lie as lightly as a pebble in a giant's palm, was
giving way, was wearing down, was losing both
power and elasticity. And the soul of the old
man was grieved exceedingly.

In the hope of still effecting good with the Irish
Parliamentary party, he consented, although re-
luctantly, to the holding of a national conference
for the purpose of settling the vexed question of
policy. While waiting for the assembling of this
conference the year 1877 passed away.

In January, 1878, the conference was duly
held. A majority of those present, as well as all
the weighty argument, was so plainly on the side
of the new tactics that the prominent supporters
of the old did not dare to take a division on the
question in dispute; and a compromise — suggested by Mr. Parnell, who did not want to break

up or divide the Parliamentary party, but only to
put some earnestness into it — was effected.   Mr.
Butt could not but have felt that he had sustained
a defeat; and the feeling was not calculated to
lighten his vexation at the course affairs were and
had been taking.   In a little while he formally
resigned the leadership of the party, but resumed
it, at least nominally, on the request of the members.   When, later on, he resigned the post of
president of the Home Rule Confederation, driven
thereto by the repeated declarations of branches
of that body in favor of the new policy, and when
on the instant Mr. Parnell was unanimously
elected his successor, the cup of bitterness must
have been filled for him, and only a rancorous or
a dull cold heart could refuse him pity and sympathy.   He had made large sacrifices of time and
money for Ireland, doing the best for her according to his lights; he had given stupendous labor
in the drawing up of Irish bills and the like; he
had devoted several of the best years of his life
with great earnestness and energy to the further-
ance of Irish popular interests in many ways;
yet, on the one hand, he found that in spite of
his numerous appeals to them a majority of the
Irish Parliamentary party, while claiming to be
truly his followers, would not work steadily with
him, and in important crises were ever ready to
split up into tails of the two great British factions;
and, on the other hand, because he was so unwise

as to identify himself completely with that worthless majority, who would neither be led nor driven to do right, he found the masses of the Irish people falling away from him and enthusiastically enrolling themselves under the banners of the men for whom his strongest denunciations had been reserved. Who could envy him the feelings he must have had on awakening to the consciousness of desertion on both sides, while he himself fully believed that the desertion on either was wholly undeserved? Justice to his memory! Even though he employed the brief remainder of his life and the remnant of his decaying powers rather in a struggle to retain the leadership from which the popular will had virtually deposed him, than in serious effort for the interest of the country of his birth and his love, we can still wish that the clay may rest lightly on his breast, in that lone humble grave in sea-washed Donegal, where he chose that his body should mingle with Irish earth.

When Mr. Parnell entered the London Parliament in 1878 his position was an infinitely stronger one than it had theretofore been. He was no longer an individual member struggling against an overbearing and intolerant majority. He had acquired something of the character of a national representative. His previous action had been sufficiently endorsed to give him much more than individual influence. All through the session of 1878, there-

fore, though he still worked in the grooves he had
previously made, extraordinary scenes were not
the ordinary result of his proceedings. On the
contrary, the Government were inclined to con-
ciliate him to a large extent, much to the disgust
of many of their stupid followers, who thought
that hanging would be too mild a fate for " that
Irish fellow." The British press still harped on
" obstruction," and Mr. Parnell was actually desig-
nated publicly " a curse to the kingdom "—the
kingdom referred to, we need hardly say, being
Great Britain.

At length, so intolerable to the British Parliament and Government had the situation grown, a
Parliamentary committee was appointed to con-
sider how best an end could be put to " obstruction." Mr. Parnell's firm position in the House
was recognized by the Government placing him
on this committee. While serving on it he completely baffled every effort made towards showing
that he and the few who acted with him had been
at all in the wrong. He also established the fu-
tility of striving to restrain him even a little in
the future, except by the adoption of some method
which must restrain British members also, and so
be hurtful to Parliament itself. In short, so skilful were the questions he put to the various wit-
nesses, and so ably did he expose the fact that the
real drift of the inquiry was to repress only such
Irish members as stood up manfully for their

country, that the British press positively took to
complimenting him, praised him for his ability,
his wisdom, and his mastery of Parliamentary
procedure, and suggested to the Ministry that he
should be often appointed on committees of the
House, where he could do most useful work, and
at the same time be kept occupied in such a way
as to prevent him from delaying the ordinary
business of Parliament.

Undisturned, either by censure or flattery, he
continued his labors persistently, amazing all, not
only by the vast number of subjects he took up,
but by the fulness of his knowledge regarding
each. There was no stopping him, because he always spoke clearly and pointedly to the question
before the House. And at last, as the days of
the session were quickly running out, and Government business was wofully behind, the Ministry hit on the sensible plan of buying off his opposition for a couple of months. This was done
by the introduction of the Irish Intermediate Education Bill, which went far towards putting Irish
Catholics on an equality with Irish Protestants in
the matter of middle-class education, restored to
Ireland a million of pounds out of the many millions taken from her and transferred to the Imperial Exchequer, and must prove of incalculable
benefit to the next generation of Irishmen.

The session of 1879 was a repetition of the
previous one in its leading features. Mr. Parnell

devoted himself, among other labors, to a continued criticism of the Government Army Bill, with the result that it left the committee a totally different bill from what it was when it went in. About thirty of his amendments were accepted by Ministers, and in the course of the long struggle he succeeded in changing the opinion of the House on several points of army discipline. Meanwhile Government business was again wofully delayed; and another bid for Mr. Parnell's inactivity was made by the introduction of an Irish University Bill—this, too, in face of a Ministerial statement, made early in the session, that the administration had no intention of dealing with the subject of Irish university education.

Out of this Ministerial concession arose a most unpleasant episode. The bill notoriously did not attempt to do full justice to the Catholic body. Mr. Parnell firmly held the view that the same method which had forced it into being could improve it in constitution. Several of the Irish Catholic members were of a like conviction, and were anxious to keep up the pressure on Government. But, alas! a majority of the Irish Catholic members would not agree to this courageous and obviously right course. Sharp words are said to have passed between the two sections at a private meeting of the party; and Mr. Edmund Dwyer Gray, member for Tipperary County, and proprietor of the *Freeman's Journal*, felt himself

especially aggrieved by Mr. Parnell through
something that took place on the occasion. He
revenged himself in the columns of his paper by
floating the story that Mr. Parnell had called those
who differed from him " a cowardly set of Papist
rats," and another story which charged him with
having used offensive epithets in regard to several
of his brother members. The first story was
promptly contradicted by five of the Catholic
members present at the meeting — all men of the
highest character, both personally and politically.
Three others, who politically cannot be said to
stand by any means so high, gave a kind of support to Mr. Gray's statement, but all three differed
materially in their versions of the words alleged
to have been used by Mr. Parnell. The second
story, when traced to its origin, was found to
have no foundation whatever. The whole country
rose almost as one man to sustain the member
for Meath under these unfair attacks, and both
Mr. Gray and his journal fell into deep discredit.
A reconciliation between the two gentlemen was
effected through the intervention of his Grace
the Archbishop of Cashel, Mr. Parnell behaving
with the utmost magnanimity in the affair.

The Irish University Act — which, though it did
not confer complete equality on the Catholics, was
yet a very useful measure— was the trophy Mr.
Parnell had to show for his Parliamentary warfare of 1879. It is needles to recall that by this

time he had all Ireland at his back, except the political tricksters and the British party-men. A striking proof of the fact was afforded by the Ennis election in the Summer of 1879. In that spirited town, so celebrated for its connection with Catholic Emancipation just half a century before, Mr. Parnell was able to carry a candidate pledged to the active policy in Parliament, notwithstanding the opposition of the bishop of the diocese and the local clergy. It need hardly be observed that the population of Ennis are among the most devotedly Catholic in the world, and that nowhere is the advice of appointed spiritual guides received with more unqualified respect, and ordinarily with more unqualified acceptance, even in temporal concerns.

Mr. Parnell had long seen how destructive to Irish prosperity was the system of Irish landlordism. Scarcely had the agitation for a reduction of rents begun than he reduced the rents of his own tenants, although, as may well be supposed, they were not rack-rents. From the outset he flung himself into the land agitation started by Mr. Davitt, coming over from the London Parliament to speak at one of the earliest Mayo meetings in the beginning of the Spring of 1879. When his harassing Parliamentary labors were closed for the session, instead of taking required rest, as others would have done, he went into the land agitation heart and soul, attending meetings in

all parts of the country. One very appreciable
effect of the agitation was a widespread reduction
of rents which retained millions of pounds in the
impoverished tenants' pockets. More valuable
still were the lessons impressed by Mr. Parnell on
the awakening tillers of the soil. Among others
he taught them that it was wrong to let themselves
and their families starve in order to pay rack-rents
to landlords; he taught them to organize and
combine for mutual protection; he taught them to
regard the establishment of a peasant proprietary
as the one permanent settlement of the Irish land
question; and he struck out a practicable plan
which, while compensating the landlords for the
relinquishment of their proprietorial privileges,
would inevitably transfer to the tillers the owner-
ship of the soil.

Finally, seeing that the British Government did
not mean to come to the relief of the unfortunate
people trembling on the verge of starvation, and
that it did mean to uphold the rapacious system of
landlordism which had driven them there, he determined to appeal to the people of the United
States. They were free; they were generous;
they were powerful; the moral influence of their
public opinion would be a tremendous force if arrayed on the side of a plundered people. To
them he would speak with the living voice; before
them he would plainly put the case of his clients.

He was commissioned by the Irish National Land League and Tenants' Defence Association.

The time of his departure was postponed considerably by a rumor, which seems to have been skilfully set afloat by some one from the neighborhood of Dublin Castle, that the Government intended to arrest him on a charge of sedition, just as it had arrested Messrs. Davitt, Daly, Brennan, and Killen for words spoken at land meetings. Mr. Parnell boldly stayed to meet the arrest.

Finding that it came not, he, in conjunction with Mr. John Dillon, dared the Winter's storms and gave up the social pleasures of the festive Christmas season in the execution of their mission. Christmas Day he spent in the middle of the Atlantic; and as for storms, his voyage was one of the most tempestuous known. One of the finest of ocean steamers, which bore him and his patriotic colleague, was, by stress of weather, delayed between three and four days longer than the ordinary voyage. The excitement throughout Ireland was painful in its intensity as morning after morning went by after the eleventh day, and the telegraph had not flashed back the news of the vessel's safe arrival in New York harbor. When that welcome news did come however, and all fear for Mr. Parnell's safety was at an end, there was a general and grateful sense of relief.

Landlordism dies hard. Scarcely had he set foot on the American shore than he found himself

confronted by a host of hostile influences for which
he could scarcely have been prepared. The cables
had been busily employed against him in advance;
a section of the press had been "nobbled"; so too
had a section of prominent and once popular Irish-
Americans. But the member for Meath was not a
man to be easily dismayed. He fronted every foe
in turn, and battled as stoutly and steadily in the
new arena as in the old. In spite of all opposition, covert as well as open, his mission must be
accounted a great success.

It is not necessary to follow him through his
American tour. Suffice it to say that his progress
was like that of some beloved monarch through
crowds of rejoicing subjects. Cities contended
for his presence; invitations rained on him;
deputations waited on him from far off places;
governors of States, mayors of towns, and other
public dignitaries, thronged around him; the
thunder of cannon saluted him in many places on
his arrival; the citizen soldiery of a free people
frequently lined his route or surrounded his carriage as guards of honor; great processions were
organized for his reception; darkness was often
banished for him by the glare of innumerable
lighted torches; presentations of divers sorts
flowed in on him — addresses of welcome, odes
and poems, floral wreaths and bouquets; fêtes
and banquets were prepared for him in profusion;
at wayside railway stations he was called on to

speak from his car ; the largest halls were every-
where secured for his lectures, and these were
always crammed ; nay, in Chicago, which has one
of the vastest and finest opera-houses in the world,
that building was deemed far too small for the
accommodation of the many thousands who were
eager to see and hear him, so the immense Expo-
sition Building of the city was specially prepared
for the delivery of his address, and twenty thousand persons, paying each either two or four shillings for the privilege of admission, gathered into
the enormous hall on the night he spoke there.
The admission fees to his lectures were invariably
as high as at Chicago, and the various halls were
as invariably packed.   Not alone through those
fees, but by direct subscription also, he received
large sums of money, which he promptly trans-
mitted to Ireland for relief purposes ; to say nothing of the fact that by his presence and proceedings
he briskly stimulated sources from which otherwise
but little was to be expected, as in the case of the
New York Herald fund.   In short, the man who
went to the United States to plead in behalf of a
starving people, and denounce the most vicious
system of land tenure in the world, had greater
than a conqueror's triumphs in his marvellous
progress.   To crown all, he received from the
legislature of the United States, as well as from
several of the State legislatures, the highest honor
it was in their power to pay, in the granting to

him of the privilege of addressing them from the
floor of the chamber precisely as if he were a
member. The scene in the Washington House of
Representatives was specially remarkable. The
galleries of the House were packed immediately
upon the opening of the doors, and the floor was
filled with members and their wives and daughters
to testify their recognition of the services rendered
by Mr. Parnell to Ireland. The Speaker of the
House introduced the distinguished guest in the
following words : —

"The House will be in order. The session of
this evening is in consequence of a resolution
adopted by the House of Representatives, which
the Chair will now cause to be read by the Clerk."

Following the reading of the resolution, the
Speaker said : —

"In conformity with the terms of this resolution
I have the honor and pleasure to introduce to you
Charles Stewart Parnell, of Ireland, who comes
among us to speak of the distresses of his country."

When the applause in the densely packed galleries had subsided, Mr. Parnell addressed the
House, and was listened to with the closest attention. His address occupied about half an hour in
its delivery, and was, says a listener, a "calm and
able presentation of the evils under which Ireland
suffers."

After the House, on the motion of Mr. O'Connor, of South Carolina, had adjourned, a large

number breasted the severe snow-storm raging to
attend the serenade to Mr. Parnell at Willard's
Hotel, tendered him by Professor Joyce's band.
A collation had been prepared by the Con-
gressional Reception Committee for their distinguished guests.   Mr. Young, Governor of Ohio,
presided ; Mr. O'Connor acting as vice-president.
Speaker Randall was also present; and, in truth,
the whole company was a distinguished one.

The remarkable honor conferred on Mr. Parnell
by the Washington House of Representatives had
but three precedents — namely, in the cases of
Lafayette, the hero of two continents ; the celebrated Bishop England, of Charleston ; and Kos-
suth, the noted Hungarian patriot, when in
enforced exile.   It should be noted also that the
President, surrounded by his Cabinet, gave an
audience to Mr. Parnell, as if he were the duly
accredited envoy of some organized and independent foreign State.   Such honors well mark
the effect of the Irish ambassador's mission.

Here we bring to a close our biographical sketch,
leaving Mr. Parnell to continue the noble career
so well begun and continued, and which we feel
assured, if life and health be spared to him, he
will splendidly complete.

APPENDIX.

SOME PARTICULARS OF C. S. PARNELL'S EARLY LIFE.

WE are indebted to Mrs. Delia Parnell, mother of Charles Stewart Parnell, for the following authentic particulars regarding his early career, in addition to those which will be found on an earlier page in the body of our biographical sketch :—

As a child he was remarkable for wit, poetical fancies, sprightliness, and enterprise.

At the age of seven, on the outbreak of the Crimean war, in 1853, he amused his fellow-passengers in the Rathdrum stage, on his way home from school, by comparing the populations and military strength of the various European Powers, with a view to determining their respective chances in the event of a general European war. Some of the passengers remarked that the little fellow had been wonderfully well taught.

In alluding to his early taste for mechanical science as exhibited in his efforts to construct a "perpetual motion" machine, Mrs. Parnell says: "Some danger attended his experiments about perpetual motion; and when he feared an explo-

sion he would call out to every one to get out of
the room, but remain in it near his machine himself." This anecdote of the boy is surely characteristic of the man ; for at least on two occasions
during the land agitation in the West, at Balla
and at Castlerea, when there was imminent prospect of a collision between the armed police and
the unarmed people, he displayed a like personal
intrepidity and a similar care for the safety of
others, flinging himself into the gap of danger,
so that the lives of the people should not be im-
perilled.

Referring to his daring escapade in the effort
to make bullets by-pouring melted lead from the
roof of the mansion of Avondale, Mrs. Parnell
remarks : "It was a great undertaking for a
small boy safely to lug an iron pot, such as po-
tatoes are boiled in, but filled with hot coals, up
two high pairs of stairs, two high ladders, the
ascent from the lead valley in the midst of the
slated roof to the top of it, and down to the coping
around the roof. To this day his enterprises are
vast, but with this advantage now — that the
greatest enterprises have the greatest opinions,
the greatest masses, and the greatest natural forces
behind them."

Ampler details concerning Mr. Parnell's school
life than we were able to give previously are here
appended : "His education, after having been
considerably advanced at home, was continued, at

seven years of age, at a small school, Miss Marly's,
in Somersetshire, England, where, while eagerly
and advantageously pursuing his studies, he fell
ill, and lay for weeks almost at the point of death,
through typhoid fever. Since then he has never
enjoyed the robust health of his childhood, and
the illness left an unnatural nervous irritability,
which, however, he has conquered. Soon after
this illness he was taken back to Ireland, and
placed under a private tutor. After this he was
sent to the Rev. Mr. Barton's, in Derbyshire,
where he again improved greatly under the care
and tuition of Mr. and Mrs. Barton, both of them
kind and superior people. Mrs. Barton belonged
to a celebrated literary family. "I will remark,"
says Mrs. Parnell, "that particular pains were
taken to place Charles with manifestly kind and
religious people. Miss Marly was especially so.
She was a Dissenter. After his father's death
Charles was kept at home under a private tutor,
until, at Lady Londonderry's instance, I sent him
to the Rev. Mr. Wishaw's, in Oxfordshire, whence
he went to Cambridge. Mr. Wishaw was a specially kind, highly educated, and accomplished
tutor. All my son's tutors," continues Mrs. Parnell, "expressed a high opinion of Charles' abilities; and the tutors of my three sons reposed a
peculiar trust in their honor and steadiness. All
three have been remarkable for goodness and tenderness of feeling, industry, patience, and perse-

verance — attributes remarkably derived." The
reader of these pages will, we are sure, concur
with Mrs. Parnell in deeming those attributes "remarkably derived." Few men had ever more illustrious ancestry.

We get a pleasant glimpse of Charles Stewart
Parnell's natural generosity of disposition, as well
as of the warmth of Irish feeling which kindly
treatment ever evokes, from the following : —
"Charles always deprecated any lack of hospitality at his early home, wanting every man and
beast that came to it to be entertained; and I
found, while I was a widow, that tenants and re-
tainers who needed it while travelling, adopted
my house as a home, as in feudal times, while,
such was the devotion of the people on our place
to us, I thought that did we require it we could
raise a corps of defenders among them. Nothing
could exceed the faithfulness and unselfishness of
our employees."

Another pleasant glimpse — one of family life
—is afforded in the appended passage : "My
children have always been good and devoted to
one another. Charles, in particular, has shown
that the child was father to the man; for the
energy and devotion he now manifests to his
country — to those who need a mighty help — are
the outgrowth of his youthful activity and consideration in favor of his family, and of his feeling,
just and indulgent judgments, respect, and un-

selfishness towards all who came near him. In
these traits, and in his prudence, he resembles his
late uncle, my devoted brother, Col. Charles Tudor
Stewart, who was perfect as a son, a brother, an
uncle, and a friend."

II.

FURTHER PARTICULARS CONCERNING THE PARNELL
FAMILY.

In the *Freeman's Journal* of February 15, 1821,
a correspondent who signs himself " C.," and dates
from "16 Parliament-street, 12th February, 1821,"
writes as follows of Mr. C. S. Parnell's grandfather,
William Parnell, brother of Sir Henry, and M. P.
for county Wicklow, to whom but a passing reference was made in a previous page : —

" Few men in modern times excelled the late William
Parnell, Esq., in those virtues which may be bene-
ficially recorded. Descended from an illustrious family,
he obtained his first literary instructions under the
superintendence of his incorruptible and patriotic
father — the late Sir John Parnell, Bart. Passing
over the scenes of infancy and early youth, I find Mr.
Parnell a distinguished student in the University of
Cambridge, excelling in the cultivation of the liberal
sciences, unequalled in chaste literature. He returned
to his native land at the period of his maturity. The
first emotion of his generous and exalted mind was

sorrow for the condition of his country, and his first desire was to remedy some portion of her manifold evils. He could not refer to the situation of his Catholic countrymen in any other terms than those of shame and abhorrence ; neither was he content to linger out his days in inactive and unprofitable sympathy.

" In 1806 he published his excellent work upon the Penal Code affecting the Catholic body, in which he reviewed, with boldness and brilliancy, the bad policy of past ages, and was the first to trace, in a manner becoming an efficient statesman, the cruel and pernicious ramifications of that system.

" In 1807 he sent forth his 'Apology for the Irish Catholics,' in which he exhibited in vivid colors the injustice of the imputations made against that body.

" He continued to the latest period of his life the same spirit of friendly exertion, in and out of the senate, to promote their claims, and had nearly completed an invaluable History of the Irish Roman Catholics, enumerating their many grievances and sufferings from the reign of Henry the Eighth to the present period.

" The poorer classes of his countrymen were the dearest objects of his anxious and earnest solicitude. He studied their wants and sustained their interests with a care and devotion almost chivalrous. His kindly heart was deeply grieved by the neglect of education to which the peasantry were exposed, and his earnest labors were daily engaged in endeavors to alleviate the evil.

" Every attempt to educate the poor could claim a participation in his patronage and purse ; and his last effort was to obtain from the Government a grant for the education of the Catholic poor on principles un-

objectionable in theory and practical in application.
He found there were objections made to the reading of
the Testament unaided by the guidance of any annota-
tions ; his wish was to serve, and not offend, and accordingly, in the true spirit of his comprehensive liber-
ality, he published, at his own expense, five thousand
copies of the notes approved of by the Roman Catholic
Archbishops of Ireland, to be gratuitously distributed
with the New Testament.

" His forbearance and consideration toward his numerous tenantry obtained a return of attachment the
most enviable and animated, the natural result of the
excellent qualities of the heart that render the relation
of landlord and tenant a reciprocal blessing.

" Possessing captivating manners, a cultivated mind,
and eminent rank and connections, his society was
cherished and appreciated by the most exalted ; but
his desire was to be useful rather than ornamental, and
he manifested the sincerity of that predilection by his
deportment through life.   He endured the most severe
of human afflictions — the loss of a beloved, amiable,
and endèaring wife — with the resignation that became a Christian, but with a sorrow that would not be
discreditable to the most dignified philosophy.   Indeed
that calamity bore heavily upon him to the last ; but
his parental solicitude was only increased, if possible,
by the additional duties that devolved upon him.

" He was a good man in all his courses ; but as a
father he excelled almost inimitably.   The education
of his children occupied a principal portion of his time
and thoughts ; these tender orphans, bearing the marks
of his care, now furnish living proofs of the excellent
qualities of their lamented guide, director, and parent.

"On Friday, the 22nd of December, 1820, he had been occupied with the Right Honorable Secretary for Ireland, in procuring through him a grant of £3,000 annually, to be vested in the Roman Catholic bishops of Ireland, for the education of their poor; and that day, on which he had completed the preliminaries to carry his benevolent design into effect, having proved unusually wet, he caught a severe cold that terminated in a malignant fever. He died at the house of his revered and distinguished father-in-law, Colonel Howard, on the 2nd of January, 1824, in the forty-fourth year of his age, being ill but eleven days.

" No man was ever withdrawn from the busy scene of life more beloved, revered, and esteemed by those who were favored with his acquaintance; and few have left behind them more acute lamentations for the departure of generous philanthropy and honored worth. One who valued him in life, pays this inadequate tribute to his memory."

The two eldest of Mr. C. S. Parnell's brothers have been long dead. One, William Tudor Parnell, fell a victim to bad vaccination, after a long struggle, in his infancy. The other, Hayes Parnell, was a most promising youth. From the age of six or thereabouts he evinced tendencies which afterwards developed into remarkable literary and artistic talent, and he was early noted for patriotism. He wrote both prose and poetry well while still a boy; and in his passion for military and naval life was wont to cover sheets of paper with original battle-scenes, and with plans for construct-

ing the best and swiftest ships. When he wished
to ascertain areas, while as yet he was ignorant of
the very name of Euclid, he drew, for the sake
of accuracy, problems of his own invention.
Although a pleurisy carried him off at so youthful
an age as fifteen, he had written a "History of
Ireland as she is to be," in which he introduced
laws of his own framing for her free government.

John Howard Parnell, Mr. C. S. Parnell's elder
living brother, who was a Home Rule candidate
for the representation of Wicklow County at the
general election of 1874, has attained singular
success in the growing of peaches on his land in
Alabama. He has been mentioned in agricultural
periodicals, especially "for having obtained by his
skill the best and largest peaches ever grown.
Their size is almost incredible." In quality they
are said to reach perfection; and the number of
them Mr. J. H. Parnell annually produces is
astonishing. He was the first to export peaches
in good condition from America to Ireland. Of
his estate in the county Armagh the corporation
of Trinity College is the head landlord. Mrs.
Parnell describes him as having more of the physi-
cal strength of Sir John Parnell, whom he is said
to resemble, than her other sons; and relates of
him the following anecdote : —

" When a boy, having received some great provocation, but unwilling to hurt any one weaker than himself,
he seized hold of a heavy mahogany old-fashioned arm-

chair, and saying, 'I must hurt something,' smashed it to pieces at one blow on the floor." She sums up his character by saying that he is "full of pity and kindness for every one."

Mr. C. S. Parnell's younger brother, Henry Tudor Parnell, at the very threshold of manhood gave practical effect to the theory of peasant proprietorship by disposing of his estate to those who tilled it. Mrs. Parnell says of him:

"My youngest son, always a hard worker and student, and delicately honorable, showed extraordinary business capacity, immediately on coming of age, in the rearrangement of his property and its sale to his tenants." The name of the estate thus referred to is Clonmore. It furnished the courtesy title of the eldest sons of the Earls of Wicklow.

III

ADDITIONAL DETAILS REGARDING C. S. PARNELL'S MATERNAL ANCESTRY.

"My grandfather, Charles Stewart," writes Mrs. Parnell, "quartered the royal arms of Scotland, which were on a large quantity of family plate he brought with him to this country; but at the time of the Revolutionary war, when the distress in this infant country (the United States) was extreme, his widow — who, besides being of

Milesian origin, was still further revolutionized in this land, and being by his death freed from the influence of her semi-Scotch husband and of the little god of love (more potent than blood) — melted down her plate to help suitably to rear her eight children, which was a matter of primary importance. This she did through the urgency of her son-in-law, John MacAuley, father of Admiral MacAuley, of the United States Navy. She was a lady of excellent education, polished manners, superior beauty of face and figure, and strong and unblemished character. All her children prospered, through her kind and yet severe training. Soft as a mother's heart is to her manly boys, she did not hesitate to punish them, particularly for the least breach of truth or chivalry.

"Her son Charles was full of fun, and sometimes of mischief. I remember his telling me how severely his mother punished him for upsetting the stall of an apple-woman — so severely that he never did the like again. I remember hearing that when his dancing master's back was turned he would amuse himself pulling out the peg (the article used in those days) that stopped up his master's barrel of beer. It was from dancing school he ran away to sea. His mother did not contemplate such 'steps' on his part. She had promised his father on his death-bed that his son should never embrace a sea-faring life.

"My father inherited from his parents, and, as I

remember, from his mother certainly, the grace
and dignity of his carriage and the charm of his
manner and conversation.   I remember the delightful stories she told and the sweet songs she
sang at ninety-three and later.   She never seemed
old in any respect.   Her husband must have been
very attractive to have captivated, when so much
older than herself, this charming beauty, and a
reputed heiress of fifteen.   She blamed some of
her family for encouraging her elopement, as they
coveted her prospective wealth, and wished to get
rid of her.   Only to my father, I believe, she
mentioned their names, she so disdained their
conduct.

"Her husband, Charles Stewart, gave half his
fortune to the Revolutionary Government, and so
helped to impoverish his family, as they never received any compensation for its surrender.   My
father, I have been told, gave the ships he owned
to the United States Government in the war of
1812 with Great Britain, and received no remun-
eration beyond what his sword brought him.
With similar devotion to a yet poor country, he
never urged his claims to large amounts of prize-
money, including those for the capture of the *Levant* and several British merchantmen, the latter
not mentioned in his life.   My grandfather, William Tudor, or Judge Tudor, as he was called,
also generously spent a colossal fortune in bene-
fiting individuals, the public of Boston and its

environs. Both sides of my family were wealthy at first, and, for this land then, immensely wealthy. Therefore, but for the traits mentioned, and had they let their means moderately take care of themselves, we would have been among the richest of the rich in this rich country. However, we have been taken care of by a wise Power, and their descendants have never been seen begging their bread. I tell the story that it may point a moral and adorn a tale.

"My father, it was said by English gentlemen visiting this country, had the most fascinating manners of any gentleman in it — a wide assertion; for none, in old grand grace, urbanity, wit, and intelligence united, not even French noblemen of the *ancien regime*, surpass Southern gentlemen in these States. But my father was descended from Irish gentlemen, under the hollow of whose feet water could run without touching them; from a race that even in the poorest looked to me, a young American nurtured among great men, when I first landed at Kingstown, as one and all, gentlemen at ease, as they lounged about with their hands in their pockets to keep them warm and clean while looking for a job. If it is true that what is bred in the bone will come out in the breeding, the Irish must have drunk, in better days, of congenial Pierian springs, and, for mother-milk, sucked honey from Hybla; for no fustian can disguise, no hardship obliterate, the keen intellect, the ready wit, the noble composure of their solid substratum, their ancient foundation.

"A brother of Mrs. Segrave (a late resident in the County Wicklow), while he was a middy in the *Cyane* or *Levant*, was in great terror at false stories told him of American conquerors, which my father noticing, patted the little fellow on the back, and told him to fear nothing. My father also paroled and helped home the crews and officers of those two ships.

" When taking some prizes into Gibraltar he was vexed by Admiral Lord Carysfort's sending an officer to one of them to investigate their business, but the officer in command of said prize threatened to cut the first man down who stepped on board. My father afterwards went to Portsmouth in England to complain of Lord Carysfort's interference, and received an apology from the Admirality. One of my kindest friends afterwards was the brother of the said Admiral. Granville Leveson, Lord Carysfort, married my late husband's aunt, and I used to fight my father's battles over again with him in a friendly way, though argumentative.

" My father told me that the great mistake of his life had been not valuing my mother as she deserved ; that the brilliancy of his career had in a great measure been due to her, and through her sympathies and influences had been destined to be

still better and brighter. She knew Latin and
Greek, and besides fluently spoke French, Ger-
man, Italian, and Spanish. Her performance on
the piano was famed in France, England, and
America; her oil paintings are still a theme for
admiration; and she played the harp exquisitely.
Her memory of history in particular was extraordinary, and her eloquence overpowering. A lady
said to me, 'Every word that falls from her mouth
is a jewel.' Her soul was too great for her means
and her sphere. Her exertions to serve others
knew no limits. Many owed their comfort, their
happiness, their existence to her; for her purposes
were never small, her efforts never weary. She
was the amanuensis of my father while he was on
the Pacific station, and wrote his French and
Spanish letters. He said to me, when he was
nominated for the Presidency of this country, that
had he appreciated my mother's abilities in time
she would have had him made President ten years
previously, 'for she could do anything she liked.'
In every relation of life my mother was a glowing
example of every virtue. Her filial devotion was
mentioned from the pulpit.

"As I peruse the letters of different members of
my family I am struck by their far-sightedness
and accuracy of detail and judgment. My mother
daily evinced a penetration almost superhuman,
and a prevision that seemed prophetic. But as
too little attention is often paid to woman's wit,

notwithstanding the familiar phrase of 'mother-wit,' she was often compared to Cassandra at the siege of Troy. I can conceive nothing more painful to human feeling than as a woman to be compelled, like some of the inhabitants of Jerusalem, to cry 'Wo! wo!' and yet remain unheeded; and I believe that life in its struggles, its future, is in tenderness veiled to woman, as a rule; and further, that so she seems meant to typify, to exemplify, the warmth and intelligence, the hope and charity, at whose pure founts the infant man may be nurtured, strengthened, and upheld to surmount the difficulties that chiefly beset the widest sphere of action — from whose purer hands he may depart winged for a double mission, like Mercury, the messenger of the gods. Woman's mission is chiefly to pity, to aid, the feeble and the suffering; and in her sorrow how wide that mission may become! History shows that, for good or evil, often, as is the mother, so is the son; and private life shows too often that as is the mother for nullity, frivolity, or selfishness, so is the son. Many a man who would respond on some angelic mission to Béranger's lines —

    " 'Plaignez le peuple, il souffre, et tout grand homme
      Auprès du peuple est l'envoyé de Dieu '—

has surely felt and acknowledged a mother's sacred influence.

"I am informed that the name Ford is of

purely Milesian origin, and am therefore inclined
to think that, as nothing has ever done so, nothing ever will quench the ardor and pertinacity
which seem inherent in all my children, the
power to struggle and to overcome, and which
succeeds in whatever field is open to it — in
whatever the hand finds to do. Let us hope it
may be accompanied too by the keen vision to see
the open door, the rift in the cloud; by the faith
to behold, while yet unseen, the blessings that lie
buried, but germinating for a greater birth, in the
Isle of Saints, the Isle of the West, the isle whose
hope, tried and purified as silver in the fire, but
undimmed still, awaits the rising sun of prosperity. 'To everything there is a time.' Some one,
some side, must tire first; and all efforts, if not
relinquished, are by practice made perfect."

The Tudors — the other branch of Charles
Stewart Parnell's maternal ancestry — have a history full of interest. They were of Spanish origin, and afterwards settled in Wales, whence
divers branches of the family pushed out into
positions of prominence, like the line of Tudor
sovereigns who swayed the destinies of England
so extraordinarily in their day. The first of the
family who is known to have appeared on the
American shores was a Colonel Tudor, an officer
in the British army. In all probability he went
there with his regiment, helping to hold the colonies for the British crown. After his death, his

widow, a woman of high spirit, disagreeing with
her late husband's relatives, boldly left them,
trusting to her own resources, and with her only
son John repaired to Boston.   Good looks have
long been a noted Tudor characteristic.   Even
Henry the Eighth, before he became bloated and
disfigured by sensuality, is said to have had a magnificent presence.   The John Tudor mentioned
above did not lack the family speciality.   He " was
noted for his beauty, grace, gentlemanliness, and
accomplishments."   Probably his widowed mother
had been compelled, from want of means, to bring
him up in the pinching school of hardship, and
that thus he acquired a close-fistedness foreign to
the family nature and habits.   Certain it is that
close he was, notwithstanding his graces of form
and manner; so close that he contrived to amass
an immense fortune at a time when the British
colonies in America, through lack of industries,
offered but very meagre opportunities for fortune-
building to even the clearest commercial heads.
He left a son William in possession of his wealth ;
and this William Tudor, revolting from the ex-
periences of his early years, and as if in protesta-
tion against the niggardliness so long beneath his
eyes, spent his money with an absolutely " imperial benevolence and generosity."

William Tudor, who was born at Boston on the
28th March, 1750, studied at Harvard College,
and graduated in 1769, was a splendid man,

physically and morally. He had in perfection what was called "the Tudor eye"—"a large, brilliant, dark-blue eye." He possessed at once the extremes of courage and tenderness, and was as unselfish as he was clear-headed. He was a very accomplished man, and a fine writer. In his young manhood he studied law, under the celebrated John Adams; but the study did not ossify his heart. Even while still little more than a boy his chosen friends were among the best and honestest of his contemporaries. While the bloody quarrel of the North American colonies with Great Britain was as yet looming in the distance, William Tudor had for bosom companions only those who might be counted on to take the side of their native country against the foreign crown. One of these intimates was his teacher of legal lore, John Adams, who, having discovered how niggardly John Tudor was in supplying money to his student son, wrote, without the knowledge of the latter, to the former, appealing to him to give William a more liberal allowance, to help his advancement in life. "If your son were infected with the follies and vices so fashionable among many of the young gentlemen of our age and country," urged Adams, "I would never become an advocate for him, without his knowledge, as I now am, with his father. I should think, the more he was restrained, the better. But I know him to have a clear head, and an honest, faithful heart.   He is virtuous, sober, steady, industrious, and constant in his office.   He is as frugal as he can be in his rank and class of life, without being mean.   It is your peculiar felicity to have a son whose behavior and character are thus deserving."

William Tudor was admitted to the Suffolk bar on the 27th July, 1772.   He had but little time to acquire a name before the revolution came.   He counted on his list of intimates some of the most distinguished patriots of the day.   There could be but one side in the strife for the young lawyer, and that side was his country's.   Of course he might have acted the coward's part, and remained neutral; but he had come of a strong and daring race, and with their hot blood surging in his veins he could not stand idle while others were arming for the fray.   He made his way to Bunker's Hill, and, as a volunteer, took part in the action. After the retreat of the American insurgents from that hard-fought field, William Tudor joined the army in a regular manner, and served under Generals Lee and Washington.   The latter made him his aide-de-camp — a fact which sufficiently attests that he had distinguished himself for bravery and coolness in the hour of peril.

There was a tender and romantic side to William Tudor's nature.   At the very time that the insurrection began, and indeed for a considerable period before that, he was ardently attached to a young lady named Delia Jarvis, whose sympathies were entirely with the royalists. He spent seven years in striving to induce her to accept him. Mrs. Parnell writes of her : —

"She had romantic ideas of feminine character, which she always maintained. Her strongly æsthetic tastes led her to prefer courtly circles; and her gentle, indulgent disposition to deprecate wars, and long for a compromise. Nevertheless she was considered to be a loyalist, and showed considerable spirit as such. For instance, when Boston opinion was all aflame about the tea question she gave a tea-party. Whoever used this herb was considered a foe to the country, and a rigid inquisition and vigilance were maintained to prevent its use. A sprig of tea," Mrs. Parnell continues, "might be our national emblem, for its familiar shape involved then a principle soon to be combated by open war."

The young lady's loyalist feelings, however, did not always go unhurt. In her son William's Life of Otis the following passage referring to her occurs : —

"After the battle [of Bunker's Hill], a young person living in Boston, possessed of very keen and generous feelings, bordering a little perhaps on the romantic, as was natural to her age, sex, and lively imagination, finding that many of the wounded [American] troops brought over from the field of action were carried by her residence, mixed a quantity of refreshing beverage, and, with

a female domestic by her side, stood at the door
and offered it to the sufferers as they were borne
along, burning with fever and parched with thirst.
Several of these, grateful for her kindness, gave
her, as they thought, consolation, by assuring her
of the destruction of [the British]. One young
officer said, 'Never mind it, my brave young
lady ; we have peppered 'em well, depend on it !'
Her dearest feelings were thus unintentionally
lacerated, while she was pouring oil and wine into
their wounds."

Courting this lady under the circumstances was
no easy task for one whom, while her sympathies
went out to him as a man, her prejudices taught
her to regard as a criminal because of his having
become "a rebel to his sovereign." Court her,
however, and persistently too, he did. He kept
up a correspondence with her during the war, as
full as opportunity permitted, usually beginning
his long letters with "My fair loyalist," and end-
ing them with "Your devoted rebel"—a mode of
address calculated to laugh her prejudices away.
Nor was he satisfied to confine himself to episto-
lary pleadings. In spite of dangers and difficulties
he contrived to meet her. In Drake's "Historic
Fields and Mansions of Middlesex" the following
passage occurs : —

"His courtship of the lady who afterwards became his wife' was prosecuted under very romantic circumstances. By the hostilities which had

broken out he was separated from the object of
his affections, who was residing on Noddles Island
(East Boston), in the family of Henry Howell
Williams. The British fleet which lay off the
island rendered it dangerous to approach it in a
boat. A boyish acquisition was now of use to
the gallant colonel. He was an excellent swim-
mer. Tying his clothes in a bundle on his head,
he, like another Leander, swam the strait between
the island and the main, paid his visit, and returned the way he came. It is related of Colonel
Tudor that when a boy, being on a visit aboard
an English line-of-battle ship in Boston harbor,
the conversation turned on swimming. Tudor
proposed to jump from the taffrail rail — which in
ships of that time was at a considerable height
from the water — if any one would do the same.
A sailor accepted the challenge. The boy took
the leap, but the man was afraid to follow."

In the end the colonel's wooing prospered. The
most bigoted "fair loyalist" that ever was could
not go on for years receiving letters signed "your
devoted rebel" from a man to whom she was really
attached without suffering a considerable abatement
of her devotion to her sovereign. Further, Miss
Jarvis had an innate horror of war; and it was
but natural that during the colonel's long absence
she should torture herself with dreadful imagin-
ings of what might happen to him at any moment.
So she put an end to her torments by deserting

from the royalists, and going over to the enemy's camp, joined her life and fortunes with Colonel Tudor's.

Honors showered on Colonel William. He was appointed Judge-Advocate-General of Washington's army, and held a military position equal to that of general. He presided over the courts-martial at Cambridge after Washington's arrival there. In his position of Judge-Advocate-General, his legal training and abilities gave him great advantages over mere military men; and these he employed with success in defence of many an accused one. In especial, a Colonel Henley, who was charged with unmilitary conduct towards British prisoners in his care, had reason to be grateful to the Advocate-General. We read: "Henley owed his acquittal mainly to the exertions of Colonel Tudor in his behalf. The evidence showed that the prisoner had acted under great provocation; but what most influenced the result was the startling testimony adduced of the mutinous spirit prevalent among the British soldiers."

When the war was over, and the colonel's sword sheathed, he returned to Boston, and to the practice of his profession, wherein he achieved a reputation as "an eminent counsellor." He became a member of the House of Representatives of Massachusetts, and afterwards of the Senate. He held the high office of Secretary of State in

1809 and 1810. He was appointed Vice-President of the Cincinnati of Massachusetts in 1816, and was one of the founders of the Massachusetts Historical Society, in whose "Collections" appears an extended memoir of him. He was an elegant and a spirited public speaker, and his talents in this line, as in others, were frequently drawn on by his fellow-citizens of Boston. He paid a visit to Europe and saw the state of Ireland with his own eyes. Mrs. Parnell says of him : — "I have many charming letters of my grandfather, in one of which he forcibly condemns from Ireland the British government there. His letters are a wonderful exemplification of his excellence and attractiveness as a father, son, and husband. He begins one letter to his wife with 'My truest friend ; ' and ends it, 'I must cease to feel and to reflect ere I cease to love and to admire you.' John Adams and Judge Tudor kept up a long and interesting correspondence — a very valuable one, being especially on political subjects of the day. In John Adams' works, edited by a descendant of his, his letters to Judge Tudor are published." The judge died on the 8th of July, 1819.

"Miss Peabody, the sister of Mrs. Nathaniel Hawthorne, wrote a beautiful account of my grandmother," Mrs. Parnell says. "In it she mentions my grandmother's resolution to do or say something to contribute to the happiness of each one she daily met; and her learning Spanish at the age of seventy. Through her letters in Spanish she procured from General Tacon the monopoly of the ice-trade in Cuba for her son Frederic. She read, wrote, and mended fine lace, without spectacles, to ninety-two years of age. Her poetry was very fine. One day, my mother, coming in with the Washington *National Intelligencer*, said: 'I have found a rare thing — a fine piece of poetry in the newspaper,' and read out, to my grandmother's surprise, a piece by herself on a Fourth of July oration, by John Quincy Adams, at the Capitol, where several old revolutionary soldiers were present. My mother was delighted to learn that her own mother wrote it. The latter was descended from some of the adventurous Puritans who sought this shelter, and the name Delia was originally Deliverance. She is mentioned in Comte de Segur's memoirs. Her home in Boston, wherein her two beautiful and accomplished daughters did the honors, was the rendezvous of all the French officers stationed near. She addressed some fine verses in French to Marie Antoinette, which were acknowledged by the latter.

"Of her two daughters, Emma married Robert Hallowell Gardiner, of Oaklands, Gardiner, Maine; and Delia married Commodore Charles Stewart, of the United States Navy. Emma had the splendid Tudor eye, and her mother's delicate complexion, auburn hair, and exquisite figure. Delia, my mother, had the Norman combination of fine, curling, coal-black hair, blue eyes, and a complexion like a tinted rose-leaf. She was tall, and remarkable for fine-cut regular features, symmetry, grace, and a dignity and elegance of carriage that were truly regal."

Besides his two daughters, Judge Tudor left two sons, William and Frederic, both very remarkable men. William, the eldest, had a strongly intellectual bent of nature. While almost an infant he had imbibed his mother's horror of war, and if any one sang in his presence the once popular song, "Oh, what a glorious thing's a battle! drums a-beating, colors flying," he would burst out a-sobbing. Ordinarily, however, he was a bright-witted and lively little boy. When about three years of age he climbed on to the table after a dinner-party, and was engaged in draining the wine-glasses when the black butler of the family discovered him. To disarm the negro's wrath the little fellow seized a glass and cried, "Your health, Mr. Pompey!" so much in the fashion of his elders that the butler did no more than grin. From Blake's and Drake's (American) Biographical Dictionaries the following memoir of William Tudor has been compiled: —

"Tudor, William, scholar and diplomatist, was born at Boston, the 28th of January, 1779. He

graduated at Harvard College with distinguished
honor in 1796; and soon after visited Europe for
the improvement of his mind. He was an ob-
servant traveller, and treasured up for future use
a vast and varied fund of information and anecdote. He returned to his native country with an
ardent desire for the improvement of his fellow-
citizens in arts and literature. He was the pro-
jector and first editor of the *North American
Review*" — the same distinguished periodical in
the April 1880 number of which appears his relative Charles Stewart Parnell's splendid paper on
the Irish land question — "which *Review* has since
become identified with the best literature of our
country. In whatever Mr. Tudor undertook he
had a single eye to the intellectual advancement
of his countrymen. No man in public life was
ever more distinguished. When a member of the
legislature of Massachusetts, he proposed many
plans in aid of his favorite object; but they met
with opposition from those who, though they respected his motives, considered him a visionary.
Several of his projects have, however, since been
accomplished, and in the very manner that he first
suggested. For two years he wrote all the first
pages of the *North American Review* himself.
According to himself, he wrote the whole of the
first number, even to the notices, etc., in it. He
had previously aided in founding the Anthology
Club, publishing his European Letters in their

magazine, the *Monthly Anthology*, begun in November, 1803, continued until 1811, and supported by the best pens in Boston. In November,
1805, he founded the ice-traffic in tropical climes
as the agent of his brother Frederic, which has
grown to be an important branch of commerce;
and he was afterwards engaged in other commercial transactions in Europe, requiring ability and
address. Mr. Tudor was the originator of the
present Bunker's Hill Monument, and one of
the founders of the Boston Athenæum in 1807.
In 1823 he was named consul at Lima, Peru;
and in 1827 was appointed *charge d'affaires* at the
court of Brazil, where he negotiated a treaty, the
last of his public works. Mr. Tudor acquired
the personal affection of the Emperor, and the
respect and admiration of the *corps diplomatique*.
His character as a literary man and an accomplished gentleman had preceded him; and it was
well observed that his country was honored in
such a representative. Besides his contributions
to several periodicals, and his critiques in the
North American Review, he published 'A Dis-
course before the Humane Society,' 1817; 'Letters on the Eastern States,' 1820; 'Miscellane-
ous,' 1821; 'Life of James Otis,' 1823; 'Gebel
Teir,' 1828. He died at Rio Janeiro, the 9th of
March, 1830." He was only in his fifty-fourth
year then; and he succumbed to an illness which
had its origin a great many years before in an act

of kindly humanity, when, travelling in Germany, and seeing a soldier's wife with her infant on the outside of the coach at night in a storm of rain, he gave his own inside place to the poor woman and child, and took her outside one himself. The climax of his disease was brought about by laborious journeys, on foot as well as on horseback, into the wild and mountainous interior of Brazil. Mrs. Parnell writes of him : —

"Lord Ponsonby, one of his colleagues at the court of Dom Pedro the First, said that such was my uncle William Tudor's humane and judicious advice, and such the influence he exerted over the Emperor, who consulted him on all occasions, that had he lived, the Emperor never would have lost his throne. A succeeding consul told me that my uncle William's beauty and nobility of form and feature made a never-forgotten impression on him. He thought he had never seen any one so handsome. He resembled my mother. This consul also related to me the first act of my uncle on coming aboard the ship where this future consul was — an act which in its simplicity and greatness seemed fitly to accompany his appearance. The mate of the vessel had died on board, leaving his widow and orphaned children at Callao, Peru. My uncle spontaneously and immediately gave them a home in his house, until they could be comfortably sent to their own home and friends. How few consuls thus treat their exiled countrymen! I remember the terrible grief and desolation of my mother's heart and home when the news of his death reached us at Washington. The diplomatic corps there called to condole with my poor mother. Congress had his very remarkable diplomatic correspondence published—for use and enjoyment both."

Of her uncle, Frederic Tudor, brother of the William above noticed, and whose genius lay more in the commercial line, Mrs. Parnell supplies the information subjoined:—

"Through gigantic endeavors, though often frustrated, he succeeded in restoring his family fortunes and the prestige of the Tudors for wealth. He discovered how to preserve ice for long journeys, and conceived the idea that the chief staple of New England — viz., ice — should be a chief source of profit; and he gathered a harvest of precious metal from frozen waters. The ice he sent, especially to the East Indies, has preserved many a life. He received specially handsome acknowledgments of his services from the East Indies.

"Some of the agents in the West Indies not at first succeeding, he chartered a vessel, freighted it with ice, and sailed in it himself to the West Indies. I have seen a letter written then by his tender and terrified mother, expressing her fears lest the ice should melt on the voyage and the vessel be capsized. But he went; and, like the farmer in the fable, immediately prospered by attending to his business himself.

"He was remarkable for his wit and tor his strong character, which made him, while very droll, very incisive in his speech, and very forcible in his views. He had the peculiar beauty of the family then — black hair, blue eyes, a fine figure, a high broad forehead, and regular features. At his fine place at Nahant he made prize peaches grow on a rock just over the sea, and discovered how to prevent them being injured by the salt in the atmosphere while they received the full advantage of the air. His letters are very entertaining. So also are the letters of his sister, my aunt Emma. I remember particularly her poetical expressions; and a line in one of her letters, while I was a child, when, describing a place she was in, she wrote, 'The frogs croak a bass to the whistling wind.'"